VIRA...
MODERN CLAS...
195

Mollie Panter-Downes was born in London in 1906. Following the early death of her father in 1914, she and her mother settled in Sussex.

Mollie began writing at an early age and published five novels, including *One Fine Day* (1947). However, she described herself as first and foremost a reporter, and it is as a journalist that she is best known. In 1939 she became the London correspondent for the *New Yorker*, and the 'Letters from London' that she wrote for that magazine were later published as *Letters from England* (1940) and *London War Notes* (1972). There were also two works of non-fiction: *Ooty Preserved* (1967) and *At the Pines: Swinburne and Watts-Dunton in Putney* (1971). In 1929 Mollie Panter-Downes married Clare Robinson, with whom she had two daughters. She died in 1977.

ONE FINE DAY

Mollie Panter-Downes

Introduced
by Angela Huth

virago

To
Bill Shawn

VIRAGO

Published by Virago Press in 1985
Reprinted 1990, 2003, 2009 (three times), 2010, 2011 (twice), 2012, 2013

First published in Great Britain by Hamish Hamilton Ltd 1947

A CIP catalogue record for this book
is available from the British Library.

ISBN 978-0-86068-587-6

Typeset in Goudy by M Rules
Printed and bound in Great Britain by
Clays Ltd, St Ives plc

Papers used by Virago are from well-managed forests
and other responsible sources.

MIX
Paper from
responsible sources
FSC
www.fsc.org   FSC® C104740

Virago Press
An imprint of
Little, Brown Book Group
100 Victoria Embankment
London EC4Y 0DY

An Hachette UK Company
www.hachette.co.uk

www.virago.co.uk

Introduction

*O*ne Fine Day was written in 1946, a time when Britain was struggling to adapt to stringent post-war life. It's hardly surprising, then, that reconciliation to change was the theme that Mollie Panter-Downes chose to explore – change not only in a whole way of life brought about by the end of the last war, but change in marital relations that were also affected by it. When the book came out there must have been thousands of readers, also striving to adapt to the strange new world, who recognised themselves in the main characters, Laura and Stephen – a middle-class, country-loving couple. Today the novel remains a reminder of those difficult times for those who lived through them, and a fascinating revelation, in all its disparate detail, for those to whom 1946 is merely the vague past.

Mollie Panter-Downes described herself as a reporter. In *One Fine Day* her reporter's skills – her acute eye, her sensitivity to nuance – are there in abundance, but she underestimated her wider talent. This novel is rich with hundreds of small pictures that go to make up an affecting and memorable whole: there's the easy shifting of view, the convincing reflections – elements not employed by one who merely reports rather than invents. She is without doubt a fine novelist, too.

Occasionally reminders of other writers surface in her evocative prose. *Cranford* comes to mind in her sharp but gentle depiction of a small community. She shares Barbara Pym's ironic humour in describing characters, and there are moments of Rosamond Lehmann's lushness in her charged interior monologues. But her ability to grasp a reader through means of atmosphere, mood, and philosophical reflection, rather than plot, is original and powerful.

Mollie Panter-Downes was born in London in 1906. When her father, a regular in the Royal Irish Regiment, was dispatched to be Colonel of the Gold Coast Regiment, she was sent to live with friends in Brighton for two years before the outbreak of the First World War. Shortly after her parents returned from Africa, her father was killed at Mons. She and her mother were left to survive on a small widow's pension in a village on the borders of Sussex and Surrey. A bookish child, she read mostly romantic novels, but also a great deal of poetry. At seventeen she wrote her own first novel, *The Shoreless Sea* (1923). Serialised in the *Daily Mirror*, it was praised for its maturity of style and ran into eight editions. It also meant Mollie Panter-Downes was able to contribute to living expenses – indeed, she became the breadwinner. Her second novel, *The Chase* (1925) was generally considered less good, and she turned to writing short stories for various magazines.

In 1926 she met her husband, Clare Robinson, who worked for British Celanese. She joined him for a two-year business trip round the world, and on their return they bought a house near Haslemere which was to be their home for the rest of their lives. They had two daughters, and Mollie Panter-Downes returned to writing. She did not attempt another novel, but continued with short stores and short pieces.

A great admirer of the *New Yorker*, then at the height of its fame and excellence, Mollie Panter-Downes knew it was notoriously difficult to get work accepted there. But she persisted in sending odd articles and stories, a few of which – much to her agent's surprise – were published. Then a 'reporter at large' piece, describing the arrival of Jewish refugee children at Victoria Station, prompted the *New Yorker* to employ her on a regular basis. Encouraged by her husband, she accepted the job she was then to continue for the next fifty years. Her first 'Letter from London' appeared in September 1939, and it was as the *New Yorker*'s British correspondent that she became widely famous. Americans and many others were fascinated by her descriptions of the life the British people were battling with both during and after the war. In fact, her 'Letters from London', where she stayed during the week, were often reports from the country. In constantly gathering material from her village – disguised as Mugbourne – consciously or not she was harbouring material for what she called her 'only' novel.

In describing a single day in this book Mollie Panter-Downes furnishes the reader with a whole life, as does Virginia Woolf in *Mrs Dalloway*. A considerable technical feat, this: a challenge for the most experienced novelist. In less accomplished hands it can go badly wrong: jagged, repetitive, irritating – points of view unbalanced. Not so in this exemplary novel. Laura Marshall, middle-class wife and mother, is the central character. It's in her head the reader mostly resides and the daily chaff of thought that sifts through a single mind, in a single day, is brilliantly conveyed.

Laura is one of those stalwart British women so prevalent in the war, so determined to make the best of things once it's over, when life as they knew it is changed for ever. Privileged but kindly, a keen observer of the shades of class, and yet never quite slipping into disagreeable realms of snobbery, Laura, like her author, is a natural observer. With humour and understanding she assesses the shortcomings of her own quiet life, and the foibles and strengths of those around her. She reflects on past, present and future as she waits in queues for fish: she feels keen disappointment when there are only hard rock cakes left at the baker, and she looks forward to the evenings when Stephen, her husband, returns from London.

Mollie Panter-Downes is not concerned with the intricacies of plot. The story simply goes from morning to evening one very hot summer's day in the village of Wealding. During this time there are encounters with various local folk, but for the most part Laura is alone, and her reflections sweep us along intriguingly. She is marvellous at summarising a character by way of a brief observation of a *part*, which, so acutely accurate, means we can see the whole. Miss Grant, for instance, teacher to Laura's daughter Victoria: 'In winter her attire was always hand-loomed, hand-beaten, amber beads a-swing against the jolly homemade jumper.' No further words are needed to recognise Miss Grant *exactly*. Sometimes the author employs a sharp little punch. Thus Mr Vyner, the vicar, was 'really good, a saint who had the misfortune to sound like a bore'. Every generation knows such people. We can recognise them and smile.

In thoughts of her daughter, Laura combines a mother's love and affection with a light hand. But it's in describing her husband, Stephen, that she presses the reader with a slight anxiety. Back from the war, Stephen, 'so good, so kind', works in London every day while Laura is wholly occupied with domestic and village matters at home. The faint but troubling indication that she yearns for more is one of the subtle elements that pushes the reader eagerly on through the mundane day. Without this vein of unease the unexciting hours could have cloyed.

Regarding local folk – an old gypsy, or the village gossip, or the Cranmers up at the big house (soon to be turned into some sort of institution), Mollie Panter-Downes makes sure her sympathetic eye still never loses its delightful waspishness. The only character who causes a kind of inner blush (though this would have been unlikely in 1946) is Mrs Prout, Laura's daily, the skeleton help to which they're now reduced. Mrs Prout is something of a caricature char of the kind a contemporary novelist would only sketch in briefly and delicately – not only because few such daily women exist any more, but also because to home in on their thoughts and ways of talking would be considered patronising, superior, snobbish. Sixty years ago, of course, long before the advent of political correctness, it was quite in order to afford the fictional charlady the same weight as any other character, and it can't be denied that Mrs Prout is humorously recognisable. But Mollie Panter-Downes's insistence on the good lady's pronunciation – 'kewpongs' for coupons – faintly jars in a way that descriptions of her other working-class characters do not.

From time to time we are released from Laura's head into the minds of the people encountered in her day, thus shifting pace and viewpoint. With admirable ease Mollie Panter-Downes slips into the different voices – for instance, that of Victoria, her ten-year-old daughter whose schoolfriend Mouse jerks her into a new look at Laura: 'There goes my mother. How tall she was: she had a strangeness, seen in the Bridbury street but not knowing she was seen . . . so familiar, yet so foreign looking . . .'

In Stephen's head we find the contented but faintly agitated husband, cogitating fondly on his pre-war roses, 'in those days a bob each', he remembers, but worrying about the future. 'Barring another major interruption,' he reflects,

> he could think of no reason why he should not be travelling up on the 8.47 for the next twenty years . . . he realised the prospect filled him with dreadful gloom. Sometimes in the night – he was a poor sleeper – he would lie imagining the most ridiculous things, seeing them selling the house, going abroad somewhere . . .

Laura is deeply familiar with the hopes and fears of her neighbours, and butterflies between their inner thoughts with a skilful shift of language. As for her own reflections, they are often as pertinent today, despite the rise and fall of feminism, as they were sixty years ago. 'My day is a feeble woman's day, following a domestic chalk line, bound to the tyranny of my house . . .' And she admits to being haunted by echoes from the luxurious past. 'Oh Madam, called the voices . . . The pretty, hospitable house seemed to have disappeared like a dream back into the genie's bottle.' What had happened? Touched both by regret and some trepidation, Laura is fearful of how well she can cope with the new demands upon her. She admires others who are more able. The occupants up at the big house were taking their move to the stables with equanimity. The house was already looking uninhabited. There, she comes upon 'three old ladies sat at tea seeming to float in the rich light, huddled together like survivors on a raft . . . not a word indicated that this was one of the last times that Mrs Cranmer would sit here, looking at Laura with her amused eyes. She spoke of everything but that.' (Shades of Molly Keane in this glimpse of the grand folk fallen on hard times). But Laura learns lessons from everything that touches her. The dignity of the old ladies recharges her determination to accept change with good grace.

And for Laura, struggling hard with the new life, the great solace is a profound feeling for nature and the countryside – surely a reflection of the author's own sentiments. She once wrote that the years spent in Sussex gave her 'a great love for its countryside'. This love is evident in her descriptions. Her evocation of a summer's day is elegiac: nothing goes unobserved – the 'clotted hum of bees', 'the swish of blades laying sorrel and clover in swathes, the murmur and buzz of uncut fields . . .' Her mind returns to such things and clings to them for comfort.

Towards the end of the day, reflecting that 'there is seldom the time or the opportunity to step ever so slightly out of the common round' (another feeling contemporary women no doubt share) she climbs Barrow Down to indulge in solitude for a while. It's here that she allows herself to abandon thoughts about domestic matters, and cogitate on both the relief that the war is over, and her marriage. In a 'rush of overwhelming thankfulness', half-submerged thoughts about Stephen, which had been ruffling her heart, she allows to surface. She wished he was there with her.

She would say to him – what would she say? She did not know but there was something to be said, something which was often on the tip of her tongue but which eluded her in the rush of moments at breakfast, the evening when he was tired and she was tired ... And suddenly she thought she would speak to Stephen this evening.

Such daydreams delay her. By the time she walks home Laura is full of the kind of resolve which gives significance to a quiet day. What she does not know is that Stephen, anxious and restless, wondering why she is so late, has been having his own similar thoughts on this 'consolingly lovely evening'. When his wife returned, he vouched to himself, he would be so relieved 'that his temper might flare up ... or he might simply say, for once, that he loved her and without her everything was dust and ashes'.

So the day ends with husband and wife tentatively approaching each other, both armed with resolve to change. They mean to resume the fun and the closeness that used to be part of their lives, now 'the long nightmare was over and the land sang its peaceful song'.

We do not know how their reunion passes. But Mollie Panter-Downes leaves us in no doubt that in the general surge of optimism that powers the book, their determination to re-establish important elements in their marriage will be as successful as their accustoming themselves to ungrounding change. Both world and marriage were threatened: both are secure once more.

'True is it that we have seen better days'

AS YOU LIKE IT

I

The day promised to be hot.

The village was no great distance from the sea. Hikers who went toiling up the chalk track among the foxgloves and the crooked thorns to the top of Barrow Down could see it, like a grey-blue rim to a green saucer, but Wealding turned its face away from the blue towards the green, snug in its leafiness which the circle of low hills protected. Here, the presence of the sea could be felt only as a sort of salty vibration in the air, like a watch ticking in the pocket, reminding the landlubber of his islander's destiny. The country resembled a gentleman's park, washed with greenish light from the great well-spaced trees, oak and elm and ash. On hot days the cows, sunlight filtering through leaves above, buttercups throwing up tarnished arsenical glare below, sometimes looked eau-de-nil beasts out of an impressionist painting. The gentleman's park seemed to have seen better days. Felled trees lay where they had fallen, railings sagged, hedges had become formidable barriers of dog-rose and hawthorn sprouting to the sky. In the village, too, there were signs of an occupation by something, an idea, an emotion. Something had happened here, so that the substance in which Wealding had been embalmed for so long – the perfect village in aspic, at the sight of which motorists applied their brakes, artists happily set up easels, cyclists dismounted and purchased picture postcards at the post office to send to their little nieces – had very slightly curdled and changed colour, as though affected by an unprecedented spell of thundery weather. Its perfect peace was, after all, a sham. Coils of barbed wire still rusting among the sorrel were a reminder. Sandbags pouring out sodden guts from the old strong-point among the bracken, the frizzy lily spikes pushing up in the deserted garden of the bombed cottage, spoke of days when the nearness of the sea had been no watch ticking comfortably in the pocket, but a loud brazen question striking constantly in the brain, When? When? The danger had passed. Wealding, however, had been invaded. Uneasiness made the charming, insanitary cottages seem unsubstantial as rose-painted canvas in an operetta; uncertainty floated on the air with the voice of the wireless, which had brought the worm of the world into the tight bud of Wealding. It did not know, it could not tell what to think. The big house stood empty and shuttered. The gardens of the smaller houses waved shaggily, goats were tethered hopefully on once spruce lawns, every gale rattled down a few more fifteenth-century roof tiles or loosened more bubbled glass diamonds from the little windows.

But in the early morning light, seen from the top of Barrow Down, the huddle of grey and pink and cream houses looked merely charming. Up here, man had long ago been obliterated by the green armies of fern, the invading foxgloves, the cony and the magpie. Bumps under the honeycombed turf marked the site of old shelters for man and beast where cattle had lowed and the smoke of little fires had written 'Morning' and 'Hunger' in the sky. Wealding children sometimes found old flints buried under the rabbit droppings; picnic parties munched their hard-boiled eggs among ghosts. In spring, dog-violets spilled small blue lakes in the bleached grass, followed later by the pink and white restharrow, clean as sprigged chintz, and the great golden candlesticks of mulleins. Up here, on the empty hilltop, something said I am England. I will remain. The explosions in the valley, the muffled rumbles and distant flashes far out to sea, had sounded remote as the quarrelling voices of children somewhere in the high, cool rooms of an ancient house from which they would soon be gone. But the house said I will stand when you are dust. The rabbits, less serene, always bolted into the honeycomb with the flounce of a few hundred white scuts when the echoes died down, bumping against the hills like an urchin's stick against railings, and the column of smoke rose thick and black from the valley.

This morning all was quiet on Barrow Down. The war was over. The rabbits nibbled the dewy grass boldly, and the lark rose in the brilliant air, higher, higher on its spun-glass spiral of song, knowing nothing of peace or war, accepting joyously the bounty of another day.

3

II

The clock in the hall struck eight. Stephen Marshall knew that it was right, for he had wound it up only last night, and that meant that in a few minutes he must go. He moved his shoulders irritably. Cup in hand, he was standing frowning out into the garden.

'Terrible, terrible,' he repeated gloomily.

'But what can one do?' said Laura.

She got up from the breakfast-table and joined him. Victoria, still seated, watched their familiar backs, curiously alike, her father's long and slim, her mother's long and slim. But there the resemblance ended. Her mother's hair was so curly, a mass of springing curls all over her head. Stephen's head was quite sleek, and right at the back, interesting discovery, there was a tiny thinnish patch under the hair. Victoria watched it, fascinated, as she chewed bacon toast.

'Voller's a shocking worker,' Stephen was saying.

'He's too old, poor old darling,' Laura said.

'It comes to the same thing. If Chandler could see it now –!'

Chandler could not, for he was dead in Holland. The gardener had died, ironically, in the gardener's paradise, the land of neatly regimented pink and azure and fleshy white

4

blossoms. My man's good on roses, Stephen used to say to friends who motored down for lunch on Sundays before the war. He could hear himself saying it, leaning back in the deck-chair as he squinted idly at the lovely creatures each in their separate compartments edged with box, Angèle Pernet like apricots, spicy Étoile de Hollande, the stout white matron Frau Karl Druschki, Shot Silk, the pale petal against the dark, the perfect buds proud among the shining leaves. In those days rose-bushes were a bob each. Think of it! For a pound you could buy twenty beauties. My man's good on roses, he would say, casual, trying not to reflect credit on himself for being lucky enough to own a Chandler, and from the opposite deck-chair a guest would make a polite murmuring of approval. He liked that, he had to own it, but The soil suits 'em, he would say, as though they sprang up like buttercups. And they would sit there, looking at the roses, talking idly, enjoying the hot sun – was it imagination that all the summer Sunday afternoons before the war had been hot? – until out from the house tripped Ethel or Violet, smart in their pretty uniforms, to take away the coffee-tray. He could see them now, making an entrance as though the lovely afternoon were a ballet, impossibly dancing across the smooth lawn, for ever lifting the tray in that perpetual remembered sunlight and bearing it away with a whisk of an apron streamer, a gleam of a neat ankle.

He swallowed the last mouthful of tea, still staring out of the window.

'It seems almost to bear a grudge,' he said.

The garden's vitality was indeed monstrous and somehow alarming. The rose beds had disappeared in long grass. Since he came home, Stephen had dug a few free, but as fast as he cleared them, the weeds blew in again relentlessly, twirling, creeping, choking with nooses of fine bone-white fibre. Old

Voller, coming up from the village two evenings a week on his tricycle, slowly hanging up his jacket on a nail in the potting-shed among the mice and onions, slowly blowing his nose in a red cotton square and getting his spade and creeping down the path – at the thought of his maddening slowness Stephen's shoulders squirmed irritably again. Old Voller was no match for the strength of seven practically unchecked years, when only Laura had been here to help him with a little muddling with a trowel now and then. The result was that a vegetable war to the death appeared to be on, green in tooth and claw. The flowers rampaged and ate each other, red-hot poker devouring lily, aster swallowing bergamot, rose gulping jasmine. Cannibals, assassins, they sat complacent with corners of green tendrils hanging from their jaws. The cut-throat bindweed slid up the hollyhock and neatly slipped the wire round its throat. The frilled poppy and the evening primrose seeded themselves everywhere, exulting in the death of Chandler.

The thought of so much to do and no one to do it often got between Stephen and his work in London, where he was pro-ceeding at this moment. Holding on at the telephone, he would doodle voracious caterpillars on his pad. Down the rain would hiss on the sooty tiles beneath his window, and he would think of the confounded green things shooting up, guzzling and grow-ing like mad. Damn it, he would mutter, slamming down the papers on the table top.

'I thought in the middle of the night,' he said, coming back to his chair, 'couldn't we get the Cochranes' gardener along, now they're leaving, even if it's only for two or three evenings a week? Young Porter. I don't see why not. You might drop in and see if you can fix it, Laura, before somebody else snaps him up.'

6

'Well, I'll try. Some time to-day I've got to go and look for Stuffy.'

'Oh, she wasn't back this morning?' He glanced over at the basket in the corner.

'I'm sure she's gone off to the gypsy's dogs again on Barrow Down.'

'Oh Lord,' he groaned, 'more puppies!'

He picked up the telephone bill, which the postman had only just dropped on the mat with as lighthearted a smack as though it were a love letter. So many trunk calls – had they really had them? The awful total suggested that Laura spent the whole day putting in frantic calls to her family in Cornwall, but of course there was no check up, none at all. Laura was incorrigible on the telephone, there was no denying it. She rambled, she paid no attention to three-minute time signals exploding in her ear. And through his mind shot the depressing thought that before the war, in the long, warm Sunday afternoon into which all that time seemed to have condensed when one looked back at it, he would not have had to worry about telephone bills and the paying of them. He looked at Laura across the table.

'You might,' he said sharply, 'have been a bit more careful.'

He meant about keeping Stuffy shut in, or about the telephone, or about anything she chose to take it to mean. At the back of his mind he deplored his use of that uncivil, positively unpleasant tone to Laura before Victoria, who sat there stolidly eating, certainly paying no outward attention. He remembered the amiable truce of good manners which used to exist, apparently, between his own father and mother. If they were irritated with each other, they never showed it. If they ever fought, he and his brother and sister were not permitted to witness the awful, the incredible, battle. But it was quite impossible, he excused himself instantly, to keep up any such polite appearances in these days when the child was always with them, day and night, when no starchy arm descended to remove her and give them a bit of a breathing-space, when she must take her whack, so to speak, out of the great adult bowl of whatever happened to be on hand in the way of conversational hodge-podge. He glanced at her. She was staring out of the window, not listening anyway.

'Frightfully careless,' he said coldly.

'I know,' said Laura.

She sighed. She looked across the table at him, her forehead wrinkled. Suddenly everything began to get much better.

'Honor Farleigh rang up, and I ran in from the garden to answer the telephone. I quite forgot about Stuffy and the door.'

'Well,' he said, 'it can't be helped.'

He got up, stuffing the abominable telephone bill in his pocket. Everything was suddenly, mysteriously better, as though the accumulated annoyance about the jungle of a garden, the telephone bill, Laura's bitch being allowed to sneak off and get herself in the family way again, had all come to a head and been lanced. The relief was really extraordinary. He came round the table and kissed Laura.

'I must go,' he said. 'I'm late.'

What a morning! Later it would be very hot, but now the dew frosted the grey spikes of the pinks, the double syringa hung like a delicious white cloud in the pure air. The cat sat with her feet close together on the unmown grass, and suddenly, sticking out a stiff back leg, ran her mouth up and down as though playing a passage on the flute. Summer at last, thought Stephen, and about time too. London would be an oven.

'If Voller turns up before I'm home,' he said, 'tell him to net the raspberries. We're going to lose the lot now the jays have got on to 'em.'

He ruffled the mousy fair hairs which had escaped on the nape of Victoria's neck from the two wiry pigtails. The back of her neck, he thought, was still babyish, innocent and touching. But elsewhere the world had caught up with her, clothing her in hideous navy-blue serge and white poplin, making wary the long-lashed eye. She was ten. What does a child of ten think about? he wondered. He was blessed if he knew, although there were so many opportunities for finding out. If she were a boy, he might have known. He tickled the back of her neck kindly and absently, as though it were the patch of warm fur behind a kitten's ear.

'Goodbye,' Victoria said coolly.

They heard him banging about in the hall. The drawer of the hall table was opened and shut, he muttered something, he leapt upstairs two at a time. Then down he came, stuck his head round the corner of the door, and asked Laura to pick a basket of gooseberries if she had time. 'I'll take them up to the office to-morrow for Johnson and Miss Margesson – fruit is impossible in London.' Half-way out, he looked back to say, 'Do send another advertisement to the Bridbury *Herald* to-day, Laura. You might be lucky this time.' Now he had really gone. The front door banged, and in a minute or two they heard the car coughing, failing, coughing again, and then its wheels crunching the gravel. He was off to pick up the fast London train at Ashton. The house seemed to rock, to sigh, to sink gratefully back into silence. Laura and Victoria, catching each other's eye, exchanged a small female smile.

'You ought to go too, Vicky,' said Laura.

'All right.'

'Don't forget your music this time.'

9

'I've got to pick a bunch of flowers for Miss Grant. We're taking it in turns.'

'Well, do hurry.'

The cat, interrupted in a difficult bit of flute playing, lifted a reptilian head and stared at Victoria as she emerged. She hesitated. Where to begin? She broke off a bit of syringa. Already dropping, it showered her with petals. Slowly plodding along the weedy rampant flower border, she broke short heads of poppy, anchusa, raspberry-coloured sweet cicely, a pansy, two pinks. Bunched tightly together, they looked charming. She glanced round the garden. It was perfect, she thought. They were always gloomy about it, her mother and father. Terrible, terrible, they said – as though a few old weeds mattered! She liked it shaggy, its lawns white with daisies, the golden rod and the aster making tunnels of green gloom through which one could creep comfortably. But in the grown-up world, isolated behind the glass partition, such things counted. For a moment she reflected on the inexplicable adult passion for tidying up, clipping and training, washing hands, picking innocent hairs off coat sleeves, blowing the nose delicately in the centre of the clean pocket handkerchief and folding it over – so!

'Victoria!'

'Coming!'

'The bus,' said Laura, thrusting satchel and music case into Victoria's flower-filled hands.

'If you go to the gypsy's this afternoon to look for Stuffy, can I come?' asked Victoria rapidly.

'Aren't you having tea with Mouse Watson?'

'Oh, yes. Oh, bother.' The Bridbury bus could be heard from afar, like a dragon ambling across the land, its snorts amplified by the high leafy banks of the lanes through which it was journeying towards them, full of school-children, of cottage women sitting vacantly joggling with their hands folded over their baskets and purses.

'Goodbye!' screamed Victoria, waving and taking to her heels. The bus sighed to a standstill outside their gate, snapped up Victoria, and swayed on towards Bridbury. Laura relaxed against the doorpost, staring at the gate through which Victoria had just disappeared, a sturdy little girl in an ugly gym tunic, her satchel bumping, petals showering from her bouquet, the music case jiggling by its metal bar from her hand. There goes my daughter, she thought curiously, as though she had never seen her before, and she thought, One doesn't really know what's going on. When Victoria was smaller, everything had seemed so beautifully easy. It was impossible to fail, all the flowers were broken off and bunched for oneself. But daughters suddenly ran away, away, scattering petals, waving an offhand salute. The bus door clicked like a mousetrap. They were gone.

She went slowly back into the dining-room. The debris of breakfast things looked cold, awful, as though they were the mummified remains of some meal eaten a thousand years ago. But she sat down among them and poured out a last cup of tea. Ah, how good! Now, said the house to Laura, we are alone together. Now I am yours again. The yellow roses in the bowl shed half a rose in a sudden soft, fat slump on the polished wood, a board creaked on the stairs, distant pipes chirped. She knew all her house's little voices, as she had never done in the old days when there had been more people under her roof. Then there had been nothing but cheerful noises all day long. In the kitchen, caps and aprons shrieked with sudden merriment over their bread-and-cheese elevenses. The butcher's young man came whistling to the back door, on his shoulder a clean white enamel tray, reposing on it a leg of lamb which looked as though someone had just powdered it, and eight red-and-white cutlets, tiny and perfect as though they were doll's house viands attached by glue. Good morning, madam, he would say, touching his forehead pleasantly if he saw Laura. Oh, madam! called the voices, Are you there, madam? The telephone bell was always ringing through those petrified remembered summers. A popular young couple, the Marshalls. Voices of people who were now dead cried Laura! over the wires from flower-filled, book-lined rooms in London that were now dust, the exposed tints of their freakish walls fading and streaking lividly in sun and rain. Chandler followed the butcher round to the kitchen, carrying a trug basket which he had arranged like a Dutch painting with crisp veined lettuce heads, sweet corn, white beans, and aubergine. He had enjoyed trying something new, outlandish vegetables unknown to Wealding. Oh, madam! called the voices. From the nursery, Nannie's wireless supplied a constant dreamy accompaniment of masculine sopranos and feminine tenors dealing with Junes and moons and you-hoo-hoo-de-do. Nannie's voice was heard, as Laura paused on the nursery landing, chanting, Prick it and bake it and mark it with Vee, and Victoria chirping imitatively, Bake it and mark it with *Wee*. Other children came to tea, leaning shyly against starched apron fronts secured by enormous safety-pins. The garden echoed with laughter and infant howls, checked and appeased in slices of iced cake. Guests arrived every week-end, turning up at cocktail time with dogs and little leather cases, an armful of magazines, grapes for Laura, chocolate drops for Victoria, who would be viewed, damp and delicious from the bath, in a fleecy blue dressing-gown with a pink rabbit on the pocket. They had never been alone.

What had happened? Where had they gone? The pretty, hospitable house seemed to have disappeared like a dream back into the genie's bottle, leaving only the cold hillside. Laura sat alone, the silence settled with the dust on the empty rooms, and the caps and aprons rustled their way – whither? Into factories, people said, where they would learn to assemble the bright and shoddy as they had learnt to pack the capsules of splintered destruction. It was funny to think that Ethel and Violet, who had spent their days setting things in a precise pattern, plumping the sofa cushion, straightening the little mat under the finger-bowl, drawing curtains against the wild stalking darkness, had learnt to pack the capsule of hideous muddled death. They would never come back into the tame house again. Everyone said so. Like young horses intoxicated with the feel of their freedom, Ethel and Violet had disappeared squealing into the big bright world where there were no bells to run your legs off, where you knew where you were, where you could go to the flicks regular, and where you worked to the sound of dance music pouring out continuously, sweet and thick and insipid as condensed milk dripping through a hole in a tin.

Meanwhile, here they were awkwardly saddled with a house which, all those pleasant years, had really been supported and nourished by squawks over bread-and-cheese elevenses, by the sound of Chandler's boots on the paths, by the smell of ironing and toast from the nursery. The support, the nourishment, had been removed. Now, on this summer morning, when doors and windows stood open, it was possible to hear the house slowly giving up, loosening its hold, gently accepting shabbiness and defeat. Nature seemed to realize its discomfiture. Birds hopped boldly through the front door, evidently meditating a lodging; Laura's dusting hardly discouraged the bold machinations of the spiders. As she sat drinking her tea, a yellow butterfly came in and settled on the faded plum-and-white pattern of the curtains as though it could no longer plainly distinguish between outside and in. It fluttered its wings comfortably, and the other half of the rose quietly, fatly fell, bearing down with it a shocked head of golden stamens.

Ought they to sell? Every now and then they asked themselves that, but the answer was always the same, thought Laura, for they both loved it. Stephen loved it especially, their first house, his first stake in the country; he had lived in a flat in London before they married. And, if they did sell, where were they to go? Everyone who was lucky enough to have a house was sitting tight in it, drawing in their horns, shutting up another room, or dividing with another family. Anything but that, Stephen said firmly. The house was not really big enough for that sort of thing, he said. Now that he was home, he could not abide the thought of other people's bath water running out, meeting on the stairs with forced joviality, someone else's life pressed up against one in a too small space like a stranger's overcoat against one's mouth in a crowd. He knew that, while he was away, women friends of Laura's and their children had come and gone continually, for a few weeks, three months, a year or so. They had eaten light snacks off trays, used the telephone piratically without paying for it, shared the work, and night and day filled the air with the dull, frivolous yatter which passes for female conversation. The contents of the glass and china cupboards had perished at their touch, their offspring had kicked the paint off the stairs and torn up the flowers in handfuls. That was all right while he was away, but now he was back it would not do. He was firm. His home was his own again. And things were bound to get easier, he said to Laura as they washed up in the evenings. He talked the situation over with the other men on the train, and they reported that things were getting easier. Bellamy's wife had got a cook immediately the other day by an advertisement in the Bridbury *Herald*, he would say, critically holding the glass which he was polishing up to the light.

Poor Stephen, thought Laura, watching the yellow butterfly gaily making free with her curtains, quivering and flirting there as confidently as though it were on a common gorse bush beneath the undomestic sky. He hated the way they scraped along, scrambled and muddled along, though he said nothing. He took off his coat after dinner, hung it over a chair, and pitched into the washing up. Wretched victims of their class, they still had dinner. Without the slaves, they still cherished the useless lamp. Left alone, Laura would have settled and clung somewhere like that butterfly, sipping without ceremony, perfectly happy. While Stephen was away she had snatched her meals anywhere. But now there was a man in the house again, they faced each other over polished wood, branching candlelight, the small ivory electric bell which was nothing but a joke.

During dinner Stephen would expand, glow, visibly enjoy himself. Then a cloud of irritation descended on his brow, he took off his coat and hung it up without a word. The least he could do for her, he said, was that. He fetched the coal, stoked the boiler, cleaned shoes. Sometimes the wicker armchair in the kitchen gave a loud creaking report as they worked together straightening out the mess. Occasionally Laura wondered, though she did not invite Stephen to consider, whether the chair was creaking beneath the ghost of some former cook – Mrs. Abbey, perhaps, who had been killed in a London blitz. An ectoplasmic Mrs. Abbey rolled against the faded cushions, clapping her hand across her splitting mouth at the sight of Stephen, with a dish cloth round his middle, frowning at a smear of grease on a glass. He was so good, so kind. He said little. But he was a neat man, hating mess and hugger-mugger. He could not take all this in his stride as she could.

She got up, pulled a tray through the kitchen hatch, and began to clear away the breakfast things. Stuffy's empty basket caught her eye, the blanket pathetically folded and waiting. Somehow she must find time to go and haul Stuffy back from Barrow Down. Then the gooseberries, Porter, the weekly shopping in Bridbury, the cooking – by the end of the day, shutting up the ducks and hens, putting down a drop of milk for the cat, she would be too tired to talk to Stephen, too tired to read. The print danced before her eyes, her head nodded, she fell into a stupor of sleep. But she was getting abominably dull. Stephen never said anything about that either. All those years she had existed on a nursery plane of conversation, domestic gossip over the boiled egg and the Ovaltine with Betty, with Rosamund, with Sonia, with all the other women without men who had stayed here. Words ceased to have any masculine gristle; they were purely feminine symbols with which one exchanged flabby facts about food, clothes, and shelter. In the candlelight of those vanished week-ends, the faces had turned smiling towards her – and where was this one, where that one now? If they could return, she would sit silent, or the dreadful new tyranny of sleep would come upon her in the middle of the party. She found that a book lasted her for weeks, she read so slowly, like a peasant, very nearly following the words with a laborious finger. Still going strong? Stephen would say, picking up the memoirs, the history, and looking at her with a funny smile. Ulysses had returned to a Penelope grown boring, commonplace, grey.

She balanced the tray on the sideboard for a moment, leaning towards the Regency mirror topped by its gilt eagle. The familiar face looked faithfully back at her, saying, Here I am, there You are, the Laura Marshall people see when they think of you. A bit thinner over the cheekbones, perhaps, the hair completely grey in front, though the back was still fair and crisply curling, like rear-line soldiers who do not know that defeat has bleakly overtaken their forward comrades. It was the first thing Stephen had noticed when he stepped back from their kiss after he got home. She had told him in her letters many times, joking about the grey hairs she was pulling out and then not bothering to pull any more. Everyone was going grey, she wrote – perhaps the shortage of fats in the food? But nothing has really happened until it speeds to the individual eye and bears down with pain on the heart. She's quite grey, he had thought in visible shock, before taking her in his arms and kissing her again as though she had become more than ever dear, as though he felt remorsefully that he ought to have been there to stop whatever it was that had played this bad joke on his Laura. The lost years were suddenly unbearably sad to them both. Oh, Stephen, she had said, and tears poured out of her eyes while the railway station banged and clanged, ran, shoved, opened and flowed together indifferently again round the spectacle of one more soldier and one more weeping woman.

III

The yellow butterfly rose and fluttered away, the cat got up abruptly and made off across the hall, her tail erect as a purposeful sail. There were sounds coming from the kitchen, and Laura picked up the tray and followed her. It was Wednesday, one of the mornings on which Mrs. Prout came to circulate the dust a little, to chivvy grey fluff airily round the floors with a grey mop, to get down creakingly on her vast knees and scrub the kitchen. Mrs. Prout obliged several ladies in Wealding, conscious of her own value, enjoying glimpses of this household and that, sly, sardonic, given to nose tapping and enormous winks, kind, a one for whist tables and a quiet glass at the local, scornful of the floundering efforts of the gentry to remain gentry still when there wasn't nobody even to answer their doorbells, poor souls. She was there now, panting with the exertion of the hill from Wealding, sighing, chirping to the cat, hanging a black oilcloth bag on the dresser, and popping something under the lid of the soup tureen. A little extra, brought for elevenses? Mrs. Prout was always tucking things away like a squirrel, under a drawer paper, under a lid, on top of a cupboard, tapping her nose, creaking, nodding inexplicable mysteries.

'Going to be a scorcher,' she said, plucking the flowered cotton away from her bosom and flapping it between finger and thumb, as though working a punkah upon the huge breasts beneath. 'Ever so warm bicycling.'

'The tea is still quite hot, I think,' said Laura, setting down the tray.

'Well, I won't say no to a cup.' No 'madams' flowed from Mrs. Prout. She was independent, a regular Radical, always had been. She looked at Laura amiably, for she liked Mrs. Marshall. There was a way about her, no denying it, but a vague one, ever so dreamy, always forgetting to order more salt, letting the fish go bad, letting the precious milk boil over on the stove when Victoria called that there was a kingfisher tangled in the chicken wire. There the milk was, stinking in brown bubbles on the stove top, and Mrs. Marshall crouching on the lawn, nursing the brilliant little emerald and blue body in her hand, dreadfully upset when it suddenly turned up its little toes and its pale tan breast and died, as anyone could have told her. Where would she be without Mrs. Prout? Mrs. Prout often asked herself as she knelt and creaked and banged about the house, noting that it was going downhill, getting worse every week and nothing much you could do about it. A pretty house, no doubt, when it was kept nice. But now, with only Mrs. Prout banging the banisters three mornings a week, and Mrs. Marshall pottering as best she could, it was beginning to look down on its luck, a gentleman's house which had seen better days. Wasn't it a shame, thought Mrs. Prout, Radical or no, that Mrs. Marshall couldn't get her girls back again? Oh, what a lot they were, with their bare legs and their painted mouths, afraid of a job of work, only thinking about that trash on the movies, running around and getting themselves babies at an age when Mrs. Prout had hardly finished playing with her dollies. There were several in

Wealding after the Canadians and them nigger fellas moved off. Little Nelly Bright, Mrs. Prout had seen her yesterday evening on her way to the whist drive, only a child herself, staggering along on her puny little slim legs, the heavy lump of a baby seeming too great a weight for her skinny little arms to bear. And all the Wealding ladies being so kind to Nelly and Mavis Porter and the others, smiling brightly past their bulging skirts, finding them shawls and the like, talking about the difficulties of war-time villages and so on, when what the little hussies wanted, thought Mrs. Prout, was a good hard one-two on their bare behinds. She wheezed indignantly, drawing in the tea in good hot mouthfuls, and the thought suggested another.

'Stuffy turned up?'

'No. I'll have to go over to Barrow Down this afternoon. I'm sure she's gone over to the gypsy's.'

'Well! Artful! Mostly they wait for the gentlemen to come to *them*, but not old Stuffy! Isn't she a one?' Mrs. Prout chortled and winked, throwing her stout figure back in the wicker chair. 'Do you want any raspberries for jamming? I hear that Mrs. Fowler is going to have a nice lot. Ours are going to be all miserable little scrumps this year, looks like – Prout says they're too old.

Too old, like Voller. 'Do you know if Mrs. Porter's son could come along and do some gardening for us two or three evenings a week?' Laura called from the larder.

'Couldn't say,' said Mrs. Prout coldly. Prouts and Porters lived next door to each other in two irregular, rose-hung Tudor hovels, the delight of all the artists, dark, insanitary, lit by lamps and candles, served by the ivied privy at the bottom of the garden between the beehives and the patches of sweet williams and the currant bushes. Laura, pursuing Mrs. Prout one morning round to the back door, had been startled by the sight of Prout enthroned under the ivy, peacefully smoking, a fat old man in his shirt sleeves, not visibly deranged by the spectacle of a lady appearing between the lilac bushes. He looked like an enormous Buddha, meditating beneath the clustering green berries. Grossness disappeared from the situation, and the only problem seemed to be: To bow or not to bow, to break in upon that tranquil solitude or to tiptoe respectfully away?

'Mrs. Porter and me are not very good cousins at the moment,' said Mrs. Prout coldly.

Good cousins – ah! Every now and then the Elizabethan-sounding phrase dropped from Mrs. Prout's lips as though new-minted. No, further back than that. Every now and then Mrs. Prout, tapping the nose over some bit of local bawdery, twitching a corner of the curtain away from that dark, crowded, rabbit-like existence which they all lived in that shocking hole of a cottage – Mrs. Prout made Laura remember the green track not far from the foot of Barrow Down along which, Doctor Comstock had told her, the palfreys and pack-horses used to amble to Canterbury. Doctor Comstock, sensing a willing victim for his passion, would bring old maps and spread them on the bed, tracing vanished roads with the tip of the thermometer case while she nodded and smiled and croaked, Yes, yes, I see. Keep up the gargling, attend to the bowels – and there went the jolly company, dipping down in the fold between the hills, stopping no doubt at the old Lamb Inn to wet their whistles – the tonsils this morning, by the way, not so inflamed. Yes, something robust and enduring breathed from Mrs. Prout, vast old mountain of becks and nods and lewd winks which would have needed no interpretation at the Lamb. Her gigantic varicose-veined legs straddled the centuries, her skirts blew in the air of a larger, dirtier, merrier yesterday. Laura, looking at her with sudden affection, said, 'I'll go and start the beds.'

'I'll pop up and help in a jiffy. The crocks can wait,' said Mrs. Prout.

Sharing this morning ritual, heaving mattresses, stooping, moaning Deary me! over yet another sheet worn thin as thin, Mrs. Prout became pure Elizabethan. The Shakespearian old nurse, bedding the pretty lovers, plumping the pillows knowingly, smoothing the linen in a tight band with a swollen red hand into the puckers of which the broad gold ring seemed to have been forced. Mrs. Prout savoured the intimacy of the moment, saying nothing as she folded Laura's nightgown, but unable to quell the irrepressible quivering eyelid which signalled, Faded, seen better days, but how it goes to nothing in the hand! Only a scrap of chiffong, saucy as you like. And she swept one of Stephen's shirts off a chair contemptuously, shaking him out, eyeing him with a stare, stuffing him under her arm as though she had reduced him to a hank of hair and a bone, a limp bundle of dreams and desires which she, Mrs. Prout, knew all about and had no patience with. Men! she would say, sniffing, throwing out the cigarette ash, banging the books untidily stacked beside his bedside clock as though she would have liked to shake the nasty man-made life out of their covers. All the trouble in this world, Mrs. Prout often said, came from everybody knowing how to read. The trashy stuff in books, the backbiting in the papers – did it do anyone a mite of good, Mrs. Prout sometimes demanded, to be able to read that the world was in such a horrid mess? God had started it, let God get along with it. There was nothing Mrs. Prout could do, and the less known about it the better, so she said to Prout. But goodness gracious, she was saying this morning as they smoothed Laura's counterpane, wasn't it enough to put a body off religion and such? Mr. Vyner had come along on his bicycle, sporty-looking in his tweed jacket with only his dog-collar telling you that he wasn't an ordinary gentleman, hearty with his Yes, thanks, Mrs. Prout, a cup of tea in this warm weather is highly acceptable, talking about hay prospects and strawberries, but all the time prying, trying to find out why Mrs. Prout never showed up in church, a canvasser for the party of God. Mrs. Prout had let him talk, as she would any flushed Conservative lady turning up at her door armed with leaflets showing the manly features of Sir Judd Manciple, the Member. Then, wrapping her apron round her arms, she had told him straight out that they didn't hold, they didn't believe, they didn't have any truck with. In a sort of witch's sabbath inverted creed, Mrs. Prout had stated her disbelief. Mr. Vyner, she said, as she followed Laura across the landing into Victoria's room, had not turned a hair, she would say that for him. Smiling, he had sat there in his bicycle clips, nodding his head from time to time, and stroking Mrs. Prout's tabby cat. A pity, he had said. One of these days we'll see you there yet, perhaps, he had said. No doubt, said Mrs. Prout with a sudden quake of laughter, but I won't be knowing it. Funerals and marriages – for the severing and twining of the thread she would turn up, support the mourning widow, cry Joy! and fling the shoe after the blooming bride, and listen tolerantly to Mr. Vyner doing everything proper. He could do it for her one day, being only in ruddy middle age himself, and Mrs. Prout's heart going plump! sometimes on the hill as she shoved her bicycle. She laid her hand on her big bosom, almost caressingly, as though it were a cage containing a high-spirited rare bird which at any moment might find the door open and fly away, away.

'Split her pyjamas proper again, I see,' she said, seizing Victoria's rumpled night attire. 'No thought for the kewpongs, have they?'

She looked across the bed at Laura, thinking, The child is

like her ma, dreamy, never knowing whether she has her dress on to the back or the front. Not like Mrs. Bellamy at Hunter's Lodge, for whom Mrs. Prout also obliged, smart as paint, always knowing how to scrounge this and that, managing to dress her children like little dolls in a box all through the war in spite of kewpongs. There was no leaning on the mop and gossiping at the Bellamys'; nothing ever found its way into the black oil-cloth bag and back, jiggety-jig, on Mrs. Prout's handlebars. You wouldn't catch Mrs. Bellamy wasting time sitting on the lawn, moping over a dead kingfisher while the milk boiled over. And yet Mrs. Prout didn't like her. No, she didn't!

'Pity you never had but the one,' she said to Laura suddenly over Victoria's bed.

Out it popped, she didn't know why. The thing had come into her head on an impulse of liking and scornful pity for the poor thing with her soft hands, her gentle smile, her one chick. Success, for Mrs. Prout, was measured by fertility – how many seeds from the packet, how many yellow balls of fluff sailing over mirrored sky behind the maternal rump, how many piglets sprawling on the spotted pink sofa of the sow's belly. Herself, she had buried four, reared four, all boys. From her vast skirts four men had sprung. No girls for her, mooning and spooning, staggering along on their little white shanks lugging a great child, like Nelly Bright.

'Yes,' said Laura, 'it is a pity. I would have liked more.'

'Well,' said Mrs. Prout jovially, 'plenty of time to put *that* right.'

Laura laughed obediently, sighing, thinking of the grey-haired woman leaning forward under the gilt eagle. Mrs. Prout pounded downstairs to clear up the kitchen, and soon she could be heard above the gush of water, shouting words of cheer to the cat, singing a tuneless ditty. After that, she would get the sweeper, the dusters, the tin of polish, and bang round the rooms for a couple of hours, pausing to admire the photograph of Mrs. Marshall in her wedding dress, to say Pretty dear! to Victoria looking wide-eyed, niddle-noddle, for the photographer's birdie, to toss her head at Stephen on the piano. Men! and her duster would flick over him as she moved across to finger the curtains, calculate how much a yard, picture how pretty the room had looked when it was kept up just so. All this would be locked in her bosom, to be retailed when she felt like it, at Mrs. Bellamy's, or at Miss Sewell's when she popped in one afternoon a week to do the silver and launder Miss Sewell's smalls. You're a fool, with your heart, Flo my dear, to take on so much – thus her crony Mrs. Sparks at the Leg of Mutton would chide her. But it was power, it was the draught of life to her. She could not do without it.

Laura, going to her room to fetch her purse (the next bus would be along soon, and she must follow Victoria in to Bridbury) heard Mrs. Prout's singing, and felt suddenly cheerful. The house, which had seemed melancholy as it creaked and chirruped and sighed to itself, as the yellow rose fell and the yellow butterfly settled, now appeared to ride confidently on the wave of Mrs. Prout's song. The trickle of sound gave continuity, promising a little retrenching and repairing, a shaking of dusters and spreading on of wax polish, a refusal to abandon the house entirely to defeat. Once more the mistress, Laura looked in her mirror, ran a comb through her short curling hair, and took up her bag. Ah, the beautiful morning, she thought as she ran downstairs, crying, 'Leave me a salad for lunch, will you? Must fly!' And she was off, running like Victoria to the gate. Sardonic, from the pantry window behind the low berberis hedge, Mrs. Prout watched her go, thinking that there was nothing much of her, running there swinging her basket, thinking that it was a pity she'd never had but the one, thinking that it would be stuffy this morning in the bus, no doubt, and – drat it! there went a cup, the last of the flowered ones. Breathing heavily, Mrs. Prout bent down and gathered up the fragments of white china, rose-garlanded, blue-ribboned, off the floor in her wet red hands. Oh dear, what a pity! She did like nice china, and such a scruffy lot of odd jobs they had now on the dresser. Mr. Marshall had his breakfast porridge out of a plate which had come down from nursery days – a rabbit in blue trousers was on it, pushing a girl rabbit in a wheelbarrow. And now the last of the roses. Majestically, Mrs. Prout stumped out to the dustbin, pushed back the lid, and consigned the shards to grey fluff and sardine tins. There! Out of sight, out of mind. She resumed her song.

IV

In Bridbury the ladies cried to each other, 'What a lovely morning!' But going to be terribly hot, they added as they darted along the pavements. Already the sun had a bite to it, an unusual fierceness, as the Corn Exchange clock unwound the morning towards eleven o'clock. The little girls had fidgeted, sighed, scratched their midge bites, and stared languidly out of the open windows, across the wild-flower collections ranged in jam pots along the sills, at the beautiful blue sky until the blessed bell released them. Joy! Out they poured into the playground like puppies let out of a hamper, forty little girls, squealing, yawning, stretching, and a few tiny boys fidgeting ominously in their knickerbockers. One of the teachers came round with a tray of milk glasses, Miss Holliday, who was going to be married and who proclaimed the fact with a dewiness, a slight absent-mindedness in the correction of exercises, and a half-hoop of flinty diamonds on her large left hand.

'Beastly stuff,' said Mouse Watson, who had plenty of cows at home. She and Victoria stood together, sipping, licking the white moustaches from their downy upper lips. It was too hot to play. Through the open window of their class-room

27

Victoria could see her bunch of flowers in a jar on Miss Grant's desk. 'Oh, Victoria, how lovely!' she had cried, bending her mild fair face over the bouquet, hot from its donor's determined grasp. For a second it had seemed possible that she might nibble off a sprig of anchusa, a mouthful of sweet cicely, and sit there at her desk, twitching and nibbling, green stalks hanging from her long lip. But touching the dark pansy with the white eye, she had cried instead, 'What a jolly fellow!' Invincible cheeriness breathed from her. She drew nature firmly into the cosy domesticated circle, exclaiming 'Cheeky chap!' over the feathered friend beady-eyed on the spade, stooping over the first crocus with a 'Little dear!' which made it seem to simper. In winter her attire was always hand-loomed, hand-beaten, amber beads a-swing against the jolly home-made orange jumper. In summer, this morning, she wore a peasant blouse, gaily embroidered, and a coarse blue linen dirndl. Victoria admired her clothes, but Laura, she suspected, sometimes stifled the ghost of a smile when they met Miss Grant springing out of Boots with her library book as though off the gentian-dotted grass of an upper Alp. There they stood on Miss Grant's desk, Victoria's flowers, looking somehow a little strange, thought Victoria, each flower as well known to her as one of the home faces, each speaking to her of a particular patch of the home ground, but looking lost and strange here in the stone marmalade jar.

She turned away with Mouse. The school faced down into Bridbury's main square. Standing by the wall, the children could look through the trellis at the Corn Exchange with its elegant pillars, the parked cars, the little shops displaying baskets of peas, red-eyed herrings, loaves of bread, wooden-soled sandals strung up outside the door like onions. It was a toy view of which they never tired. Through the green slats of their private look-out post they could quiz the adult world, queer mixture of stupidity and power, getting on with its incomprehensible affairs, unconscious of spies in the undergrowth. It threw them into frequent spasms of laughter. This morning a stout old woman, attached to a choking little dog on a string, nearly got run over by the Wealding bus. Some ladies met and gossiped only a few yards away, clucking like hens, scratching, throwing up their chins in funny little drinking motions towards the sky. 'Oh, my *dear*,' they cried in their silly voices, and Victoria and Mouse imitated them. 'My *dear*,' they cried in the affected accents which they assumed for all adult impersonations, and it struck them as killing, perfectly killing. They gasped.

'Don't forget you're coming to tea to-day,' said Mouse.

'Oh, my *dear*, no,' drawled Victoria. 'Oh, my dear, absolutely *not*.'

Their wit killed them again. Exhausted, they peered out once more through the trellis for fresh entertainment.

'There goes your mother,' said Mouse suddenly.

How strange, thought Victoria in a flash of calm objectivity, as though she had never seen her before. There goes my mother. How tall she was! She had a strangeness, seen in the Bridbury street but not knowing she was seen, like Miss Grant's flowers, so familiar, yet exiled and foreign-looking in the marmalade pot. There goes my mother, a very tall woman in a striped cotton frock. Mouse kept a tactful silence, watching too. Laura stood still for a moment, looking vaguely round, her finger on her lip, and then she turned towards the checked curtains of Rosemary's Tea Shoppe. If only we could be at the sea to-day, thought Victoria, just the two of us, swimming and splashing, eating hard-boiled eggs and lettuce among the sand dunes. Oh, how hot it was! Laura had passed from sight. In a few minutes, thought Victoria, irritably scuffing her heel into the flower bed, the bell would ring.

V

A cup of coffee, Laura had been thinking while she stood hesitating, and then I can catch the bus home at half-past eleven. The shops, she observed, had a bare, denuded look, as though locusts had descended. Every morning clouds of women came down from the little Georgian houses and snug cottages of Bridbury, they poured in from the surrounding villages, they stripped the counters bare. After eleven, for those in the know, the little town had nothing much to offer. Sorry, the shaken heads would signal to those foolish virgins who came late with their baskets to seek the rare orange, the spotted plaice, the yellow and unyielding bun. But still little Bridbury looked very pretty and prosperous in the sunshine, the new white paint of the Bull glistening, the dark-brown leather and silver bits in the saddler's shop gleaming, and suddenly, round the corner, a drove of sheep being driven to the market, jostling, chins high in panic on each other's dirty woolly backs, filling the air with their country bleating.

Laura's arm ached, for her basket was heavy. She turned thankfully into the coolness of Rosemary's Tea Shoppe where, an hour earlier, she had been queuing for cakes. Now the wire trays on the counter were empty; the locusts had been and gone. About a dozen other women and one or two stray men, who looked uneasy, as though they would have been happier at the Bull, sat about at the small tables, drinking coffee and eating soggy buns. Everything here which was not curly wrought iron was bulbous polished brass or copper, the beams ran whimsically crooked, the window panes distorted the light in greenish spirals. The young woman in the flowered smock advanced, patting her back curls, looking at Laura with pronounced disgust.

'Coffee?'

'Yes, please.'

'Bun or rock keek?'

'Rock cake, I think.'

How much wiser to say neither, but the flesh was weak, the flesh craved the filling wad of starchy substance. 'Home-made cakes,' announced the dainty hand-painted card, ornamented with a pixie squatting on a scarlet-spotted toadstool, and painfully home-made they were, quite distressingly wholesome. 'Cakes nowadays are not worth the buying,' her neighbour in the queue, a large woman in a hot-looking tomato-red dress, had said to Laura, but there she had waited, there Laura waited, there they all waited on the hot pavement. Other women, not needing cakes to-day, passed by and looked at them disdainfully. A lorry load of soldiers, seeing skirts, raised the instinctive lustful whistle as they roared past. A moth-eaten Cairn terrier and a black mongrel started a fight, and were jerked apart by their warm, irritable owners. 'It's difficult feeding the doggies to-day,' the tomato-red woman remarked to Laura. 'My sister has quite a game getting the horse meat for her little terrier. Oh, he's so intelligent! He stands there with her in the queue, and "Bark for it!" she says to him –' The Corn Exchange clock struck ten, at which hour Rosemary would unlock her Shoppe. The queue quivered, craning their necks, hoping for a whisk of flowered smock between the checked gingham curtains. 'Every morning he brings my sister his little brush and comb,' Laura's neighbour was droning. Joy! The long line was moving. 'But she doesn't spoil him – oh no! He's allowed his own little rug on the sofa, but if he gets up on a chair, my sister says to him –' The dreadful loneliness and poverty of people, reduced to bragging about the engaging ways of their sister's little doggie. Dreadful, dreadful, thought Laura, feeling sudden acute pity for the stout tomato-red party, acute pity for herself having to stand waiting to buy a slab of vile cake from a Rosemary whose ways were so much less old-world than her Shoppe, who would snap, Not more than *six* tea keeks, sorry, her eyes hard with dislike of all these old women trying to put one over, of all these bloody warming-pans, of stick-in-the-mud Bridbury. Somewhere, at this moment, the blue grass waves, in the middle of the jungle rise the soft old grey ruins carved with blind smiling faces, the white bird flies out of the scarlet blossoming tree. Here we stand, however, the baskets limply in our hands, waiting for Rosemary to give us not more than six tea cakes. Not so far away, thought Laura, is the sea, but how many times had she been there this summer? On such a perfect day she should have sent the house, Mrs. Prout, Stephen's dinner, Stuffy's whereabouts, all the complicated little pieces of her everyday humdrum, round to the four winds of heaven. She should have kept Victoria from school, cut sandwiches, hunted out the bathing-things, and away they should have gone. On this side of the hills, the air lay like a quilt of feathers on the tops of the heavy trees. But as the bus took them towards the sea, the face of the land would change. The trees bent all one way, seagulls flapped over the stony plough, the little farms looked bleached and scrubbed by the salt air. Rounding the corner of a high flint wall, Victoria always said Look! and there was the old ship's figurehead propped up in the cottage garden, a high-bosomed woman with the blank blue eyes of the sea king's daughter, and behind her on the window ledge a row of enormous spiked pink shells. Perhaps, eating their sandwiches among the coarse quivering grasses on the sand dunes, the word would be said, the mysterious pass-sign would be found, which would take her and Victoria back to their lost country . . . Yes, to-morrow, she thought, to-morrow we will do it. This weather is going to last for a few days. London must be awful, she thought, pitying Stephen. The war is over, Stephen was not killed, we could still live like gods, but he sits in his hot office, and here I stand. Is there any sense to it? Meekly she had held out her basket to Rosemary, the goal, the summit triumphantly reached at last.

'No tea keeks left, sorry,' said the glacial voice from the summit. 'Only buns and seed keek.'

Seed cake, oh horrors! 'But I'll take one,' she had replied, while the young woman dumped the slab into her basket and stood waiting for the money, her fingers winding and unwinding one round curl of her new permanent, her eyes staring indifferently past the warm fidgeting line of women, out into the sunshine. 'Seed, I can't eat seed,' the tomato-red party was saying like a disgruntled canary to whoever might be listening.

The coffee appeared now, a small lump of sugar in the saucer, with the rock cake, craggy, unhopeful, a very Gibraltar of confectionery. Laura bit and swallowed without enthusiasm. Eating had become just that – biting and swallowing. She had never been a greedy woman, but toothsome ghosts of food kept on floating back from the past – now, for instance, chewing the negative wholesomeness, she found herself remembering some

34

delicious little rum-flavoured cakes which she and Stephen had eaten somewhere abroad on their honeymoon. Where? She could not remember, but there had been cool columns of a piazza framing green and purple sea, some elderly men playing chess and reading newspapers in their shirt sleeves, a piano and a violin playing Verdi, flies buzzing, and of course those delicious little poems of cakes. Her mouth watered at the thought, as it was always watering, taken by the mind on a sort of Baedeker tasting-tour of Europe. In the shadow of a great, grave French cathedral, a pale girl done up in two-inches-deep black like a mourning envelope had weighed out chocolate truffles in a charming little pale blue carton. Alas, she could remember nothing of the cathedral, its glass, its superb treasures, but she could remember every melting brown mouthful of those truffles. In the little inn among the forests of Spanish chestnuts, the old man had cooked the dinner, sitting down to eat it at the next table, vast and pink-skinned in his chef's apron. The forests had withered in her memory, but how clearly she recalled the trout, the chicken, the wood strawberries in their vine leaves. Of course she was lucky to be sitting here, she chided herself, eating this good filling rock cake. What has happened to the pink-faced old man now, to the pale girl already buttoned up in inky black as though dedicated to loss and sorrow? Yet her mind refused to follow the humble, thankful path. Like a naughty dog it slunk away, guilty, drooling on the scent of the rum of yesteryear. Yes, there was no doubt, she had become a greedy woman. From her honeymoon, a time of great happiness, she could salvage only a few paltry cakes. As for Victoria, she lived for food. At school the little girls boasted and bragged, chinking the small change of the extra orange, the rare iced cake, which life would harden later into the currency of the better motor-car, the more satisfactory husband. And I assist her,

35

thought Laura sadly. When Mrs. Prout turns up, winking, sighing There's bananas in the village, do I not drop everything, leap for the bicycle, arrive panting at the shop, agonized with fear in case Victoria shall be the only child at Miss Grant's not happily peeling one of those overrated things?

Good heavens! she thought, I must fly for the bus. She jumped up and went over to the counter where the young woman was leaning on one fingertip as though gloomily testing its staying power.

'How much is that?'

'Eet-pence, with one keek.'

Counting out sixpence and two coppers, Laura said, 'What a lovely day,' suddenly perversely anxious to see the girl smile, melt, look down from the high window of her Shoppe on Camelot. 'Nice if you're out, I dare say,' Rosemary observed. But she smiled. The mirror cracked from side to side, she became human, admitting the warm impeachment of flesh and blood under the flowered smock. Was it possible that she might have a last fruit cake hidden in a warming-pan? Laura heard the bus rocking down the square, stopping in front of the Bull's geranium-filled window boxes where it would sit and snort meditatively for two minutes only. There was no time to follow up the opening. She ran.

VI

The bus was full of women, sighing, sweating gently under the arms of their cotton dresses as they held on to their baskets and their slippery, fretful children. A tiny boy screamed like an angry jay, drumming his fists on the glass. He wa-anted it, he wa-anted it! Bless the child, wanted what? It, it, ow-w-w! he wept with fury at adult stupidity already frustrating his simple world. A spaniel on the floor at somebody's feet shifted cautiously, lifting a red-cornered eye towards his owner, hoping and trusting that no one would tread on his paw. Human uneasiness and irritability seemed to fill the bus with hot cottonwool, choking, getting up the nostrils. If it did not start in a moment, it might burst with pressure from its prickling cargo. Only a young man, a hiker, seemed to sit aloof and happy in the heat. He wore a blue shirt and drill shorts; on his knees was a knapsack. His neck was a dull red, so was the brow of his cheerful, ordinary face. Perhaps he had only just come out of the Army or the Air Force, thought Laura, watching him study his map with such happy concentration. Ow, ow, ow-w-w, wept the tiny boy, unable to escape and go striding off amongst the bracken, still handcuffed to childhood. I'll smack you proper if you don't stop, threatened his mother. The young

37

man studied his map, reading England with rapture. The driver, who had descended to cool his legs and have a word with a crony outside the Bull, swung himself up into his seat. An angry throbbing seized the bus, the hot bodies of the passengers quivered like jelly, the jaws of an old woman by the door seemed to click and chatter. With a lurch, they started. The tiny boy's tears stopped as though within his tow-coloured head someone had turned a tap. His brimming eyes stared out at the streets as he sat quietly on his mother's lap, clutching a little wooden horse.

They rounded the Corn Exchange, tooting imperiously at a red-faced woman driving a shaky old trap, a vast flowered hat skewered to her head, a couple of sacks beside her. There was Victoria's school, a pleasant Georgian house with a magnolia up its front wall; as usual, a nostalgic trill of piano music whiffed through its open windows. Somewhere in there, thought Laura, she is droning away, having her head crammed with stuff, serving out her sentence. To-morrow, yes, to-morrow we'll cut and run to the sea, Victoria. The bus trundled down the narrow street. The little bow windows leant towards it, poising a jungle of puce and crimson pelargoniums, a canary in a cage, an old man reading the Bridbury *Herald* in a rocking-chair. I've forgotten that advertisement, thought Laura penitently. Oh dear, Stephen, I've forgotten that advertisement for a cook. But I can post it, she comforted herself, although no one will answer it. Only Stephen still believed that someone would answer it. The bus rounded a corner, and they all rolled gently against one another, eyeing each other's baskets, wondering what she had got that I had not got. Was that a lemon? A bit of liver spreading damp brown patches on the wrapping newspaper? Too late now, anyway. Bridbury was vanishing. The last houses, the South Hills Garage, the Duke of York, a dark little pub without the Bull's geranium-filled window boxes, catering to the railway porters and van drivers and to thirsty commercial travellers coming off the train – and now the bus dived into the close green channels of the lanes. The passengers relaxed, the fret of the morning over, its trophies in string bags and baskets on their knees, its mistakes fading from their minds.

'Twelve little ducks the husband got,' the woman behind Laura was saying.

'Fancy, now! We had no luck.'

'Yes, twelve, twelve beautiful little ducks under the old Rhode Island.'

'Was the strawberries good this year?'

'Middling, if it weren't for slugs.'

Comfortingly the country talk started and sighed to a standstill with the bus. Bridbury had been hot, you could not buy a thing you wanted, people were rude. They were returning pilgrims who had sustained great dangers, who could tell a tale, who were glad now to be back. Every now and then the bus stopped and set down one or two women, who walked slowly away, their arms dragging with the weight of their bundles, towards the cottage gate and the little porch loaded with honeysuckle or rose. And now came a gap in the high banks. The heat shimmered on the sea of bearded green, eared yellow, shivering grey, lapping right up to the rough fringe and chalk pits at the foot of the low hills. Barrow Down reared its head, crested with fern and foxglove. The young man with the map leant forward. The war was over, over, thought Laura. At odd moments, with queer moving force, the thought recurred so that one thought, Thank God! A year ago no young men in blue shirts went striding off on a summer morning to assault the peaceable, rabbit-guarded strong-point of Barrow Down. He glanced her way, ducking his head to see something on her side of the bus, and, catching his eye, she smiled warmly. Was she really smiling at him? Warily he averted his eyes, and the back of his neck flamed a little deeper. He was a nice young man, he had a pocket Keats in his knapsack. He read his map studiously. At the next stop, the cross-roads where one lane wandered off to Grimsditch and the other started to mount steeply between hedges of dog-rose towards Barrow Down, he got off and stood hitching his knapsack over his shoulders. Then, giving himself a little shake as though divesting himself of his last contact with sticky, peevish humanity in the bus, shaking them off as a dog shakes pond water from his coat, he started to walk at a good sober, soldierly pace up the lane. He walks alone by choice, thought Laura. He walks with calm, manly decision, while my day is a feeble woman's day, following a domestic chalk line, bound to the tyranny of my house with its voices saying, Clean me, polish me, save me from the spider and the butterfly. It is so long since I measured out a day for myself and said, This is mine, I shall be alone. Men are so much wiser, she thought, striding deliberately off, shaking the press of other people from them and climbing the lonely hill. One day soon, she promised herself vaguely as the bus passed the first cottages of Wealding.

She would get off at the church, the other end of the village, and call in at the Porters' cottage on her way home. At the Leg of Mutton, several people got out, the hot air changed and soaked up new smells as new people climbed in. The spaniel smell, armpits, onions went, and were replaced by sweet peas, more armpits, and old Voller, clambering aboard and sitting down very suddenly beside Laura. He smelled strongly of earth, like some tiny, antique animal who lived in a bank. His hand, lifting a red cotton handkerchief to mop his forehead, was a knobbly collection of knuckles, earth-darkened and spatulate, but his wrist was thin, blue-veined, touching as a child's.

'Terrible warm,' he said. A ghost of a voice whistled from Voller like wind through a keyhole.

'Going to see my darter at Gospel Oak,' came the fluty little keyhole voice.

'Will you be able to come along this evening, then?' shouted Laura. He was deaf as an adder, poor old Voller. Only the keyhole of sound and hearing remained through which he could receive crumbs and drops of the world, a prisoner, walled up in that frail, brittle, ancient body. He nodded. He would come along. The raspberries, Mrs. Marshall said, would he net the raspberries? That, too, was pushed through the keyhole, and back came the little shrill whistle. Oh yes, he would net them. If he netted himself, the birds would see no difference. He would bud, he would blossom, his toes would take root in England, his fingers would splay down comfortably into the soil.

'Good,' shouted Laura, smiling and nodding down at him as she got up to go. Poor old Voller; she felt guilty, going off now to see if she could not get a lusty young Porter to supplant him. Was the daughter at Gospel Oak kind to him? Laura knew her by sight, a big fresh woman like a horse dressed in blouse and skirt. Incredible to think that she existed owing to an impulse of old Voller's! Over his head loomed the shadow of the Institute, the yellow brick building on the hill where the old people crept in the sun, eking out the week's little wad of tobacco, meekly eating the bread of charity and idleness. In the Institute garden grew nothing, it seemed, but rhubarb and cabbages, sharper than the tooth of a horse dressed in blouse and skirt, watery with the water which would turn out in the end to be thicker, more dependable, than blood. She would talk to

Stephen to-night, thought Laura, working with her basket past the fat knees, the bundles, the squirming children, towards the fresh air. Even if George Porter can come to us, we must keep on old Voller. She got out of the bus, feeling its hot exhaust fan out at her as it moved off.

The calm of Wealding enfolded her. Now Bridbury was the dream. The clock said See-saw four times, immediately striking twelve reticent notes. For what it is worth, it seemed to say, the hour is noon. The midday sky had the sheen of a tightly stretched width of royal-blue silk. A high insect hum came from the long grass and moon daisies of the churchyard. The shirt of the young man climbing Barrow Down, thought Laura, must be sticking to his back. She pushed open the cottage gate, descended a deep step between rows of lilies, and walked round to the Porters' back door. Roses poured down from the crumbling cottage wall, wreaths and swags of crimson and pinkish yellow. The lilies were magnificent. Mrs. Porter gave them little attention beyond tipping out a pot of tea leaves round them now and then to keep off the blight; the little Porters made water against a row when they felt inclined. But they were superb white tapers, thickly clustering, heavy with bees. No one in Wealding had such phloxes. Everything grew here in this patch of damp black soil, worked for generations. At the back door Laura paused, glancing at a pair of old boots, a child's battered tricycle upside-down in the path, the privy open as usual beneath the ivy. No one sat there to-day, no Prout, no Porter. A hen throatily clucked, scratching among the currant bushes.

She knocked.

VII

They were inside, eating dinner. She had banked on catching them at home now. Someone put down a fork on a plate, there was the silence of people listening with their mouths full, and then Mrs. Porter opened the door, wiping her lips with her fingers, crying, 'Oh, good afternoon, m'm. Excuse me not asking you in, m'm – we're having a bit of dinner.' She edged herself out, half-closing the door, so that all Laura could see was a patch of damp wall and a calendar depicting two grey kittens sitting in a man's boot. Inside, the eating noises began again.

'Summer weather at last, m'm,' said Mrs. Porter, smiling, looking Laura up and down. The respectful address escaped her continually like a soft hiccup. She was no Mrs. Prout, she recognized the gentry even if they were going through difficult times. The 'm'm' bubbled from her as though from a deep old spring. Her smile revealed shocking teeth, blackened ruins tumbling one upon the other, but her dirty dress was a cheerful blue, the colour of a sugar bag; in her improbable yellow hair, grips and bits of rag bristled like leeches, but would later be drawn off and replaced by a jaunty, grubby blue bow. One of these days, she often said, she would go to Doctor Comstock and find out about getting a fine new set of teeth. Her dirty feet, veined with purple nodules, were thrust into broken-down evening shoes. She smiled at Laura, respectful, slippery, false as a cat. She was a light one, all Wealding knew it. When the Army were here, she was seen smoking cigarettes, drinking at the Leg of Mutton, larking in the fields with soldiers young enough to be her son. A fat corporal named Tuck was for ever hanging round the cottage. Mrs. Porter sat on his knee, Mrs. Prout had reported to Laura, with Porter looking on, a dummy in his own chimney corner. Shrieks and giggles and slaps had floated out from among the roses. After Tuck left, she took up with a Canadian, a nice young fellow. The men of the Observer Corps, sitting waiting for Heinkels on Barrow Down, had seen the blue dress frisking spryly among the bracken, the khaki patch following after, khaki and blue sinking from sight among the fronds, sinking, drowning from sight in the green breakers, not rising again. It had relieved the tedium of their afternoon nicely, Mrs. Prout had implied, winking, tapping her nose as she stood at Laura's sink.

'I was wondering –' began Laura.

'Yes, m'm,' said Mrs. Porter, her light blue eyes sliding with false humility over Laura's dress and face.

A chair squeaked along the floor in the dark little room behind her. How many there? Laura had lost track of the Porters long ago. George, the eldest son, was back from the war. One of the elder girls, Dolly, looked after old invalid Mrs. Grant in the village. Mavis Porter had come to grief, light, like her mother. She had gone off in the W.A.A.F.s and come back with a child, fathered by a Pole. Married, of course, with a wife and family out there somewhere, Mrs. Prout had reported to Laura with a gale of sniffs. Men! she had cried, whacking the soap powder into the washing-up water in a frenzy of contempt.

No doubt he had kissed hands, quite the foreign gentleman, taking in poor Mavis who was a nice girl though not really strong in the head. Men! Mrs. Prout had snorted, shaking them violently out at the back door with the dusty floor mat. And really, Laura had reflected, it was queer to think of Poland stretching out to meet the Porters, the strange distant city planting a son here beneath the thatch and the rats of this slatternly roof. Mavis Porter's son would open his eyes to no crowned and gentle Virgin, but to two grey kittens in a man's boot. The chimes would not wing their way like grave birds from the lofts of bronze cupolas and stone towers through the night, but the English clock would say See-saw kindly to him at intervals across the churchyard.

Yes, Mavis was here, George, Dolly, but of the younger Porters Laura could not keep account. Mrs. Porter threw them off so lightly. The blue dress bulged, it clung concavely again, and again a bundle lay in the old pram outside the back door. Between bouts in the bracken, Mrs. Porter always had a child in her arms, and she loved them all, she named them so ambitiously. Victoire, the one who was born when the bonfire flared on Barrow Down, had been named, and goodness only knows, Mrs. Prout had said tartly, whether it was going to look like a fat corporal or a thin Canadian. Goodness only knew, Mrs. Porter did not. She enjoyed life, she took what came. The evening shoes, the afternoon bow which would follow the morning curlers sucking the life from her yellow hair, were somehow pathetic, Laura thought. She remembered how once before at this back door, when she had called on some errand, Mrs. Porter had suddenly, abruptly said Come in, and drawn her into the kitchen and disappeared upstairs. Laura heard her run-over high heels slopping across the floor overhead, a drawer being opened and shut, and then back she came, clasping a box. She took out of it a small orange silk tablecloth, painted with a view of the Bay of Naples, very blue, looking exactly like a bay, and Vesuvius puffing clouds of Chinese white. She shook it out carefully, watching Laura's face. Hand painted, she said. Ever so pretty, isn't it? Ernie got it when he was overseas in the last war. It's lovely, Laura said. Looking at her tablecloth, Mrs. Porter's face became vacant, remote, faintly bewildered. Thus should life be, the strangeness of the foreign city, the bright silk, the brilliant sky and water, love with a dark stranger in one of those little boats bobbing about so realistically. Thus should life be, insisted the blue hair-bow, the rouge in hard patches on the thin cheekbones, the slaps and giggles of an evening, the perpetual Gold Flake hanging from the lips. Luckier women kept their poetry in thin volumes on the shelf. Mrs. Porter kept hers folded between tissue paper in a drawer. The impulse to show it to Laura had been sudden and inexplicable. Smoothing the Bay of Naples back into its box, her eyes had begun to slide shiftily again, her face to resume its usual expression of feeble brightness . . .

'Yes, m'm,' she was saying now, while an infant Porter suddenly appeared at her skirts, straddling on bandy legs, smiling shyly at Laura with a messy mouth. 'Colonel Cochrane is leaving. Going to live near his sister in Ireland, isn't he, m'm? No, he hadn't said nothing to George about the new people taking him on.'

'Then do you think –' asked Laura.

'George!' called Mrs. Porter over her shoulder.

'Don't disturb him if he's at his dinner,' said Laura.

'Oh, he's just about finished, m'm. Meals don't take so long nowadays, do they? It's a job!'

Now appeared George Porter behind his mother, the first-born, the opposite end of the line from the tiny creature swaying beside the blue skirt, showing its bare tail beneath its petticoats as it nearly lost its balance. He wiped his mouth with the back of his hand, grinning. Laura had not seen him since he got out of the Army. Before that he had been one of the boys of the village, shambling about in gangs, hanging over walls on Sundays to see the cars go by to the coast. Good gracious, thought Laura, what a magnificent young man he has become. Masculine beauty is now so rare, tamed into a genteel quality known as 'attractive,' that the occasional authentic bright gleam takes away the breath. Thus should men be, stated George calmly, emerging in his splendour from the poky dark cottage, springing like a god from the union of a woodman who could hardly read and a slut. Had Mrs. Porter wandered into the bracken in her youth with a handsome stranger? But no, there was an unmistakable reminder of his father about the chin, just as there was something of his mother in his blue eyes, but all refined, gilded with immortal powder. Here is Mrs. Porter's Bay of Naples, thought Laura, suddenly stammering as she realized that they were waiting for her to speak, and there she was, caught staring, dreaming as usual.

'Well,' said George reflectively when she had finished.

He looked at her amiably, as though she were a nice sofa. That must be the penalty of the grey hairs, the tired shadows under the eyes, that must be the beginning of getting old. She had noticed it. Young men looked at you as though you were a nice sofa, an article of furniture which they would never be desirous of acquiring. The signal flags were hauled down, the lights went out, all commerce between the sexes to cease forthwith. Certain faithful, seasoned admirers remained loyal. Philip Drayton, now a dignified K.C., a terrific swell, still remembered to send the right flowers (lilies of the valley) on the right days with the old card,

'For Laura – Phil.' Yes, she thought fretfully, while with placid face she stood talking to the Porters, yes, indeed, was not Doctor Comstock particularly gallant when they met in the village, twinkling at her out of his old Vauxhall, saying, No need to visit you on my round, I can see that, Mrs. Marshall! Did not even Mr. Tubbs, the butcher, revive when she came in, sparkle and crack a joke and become a dog, leaning forward tenderly to whisper, even though they were alone in the shop, Would you like a tail? diving into the cold room and returning to place the precious oxtail in her basket as though he alone, for her sweet sake, had hacked it off the infidel in the Holy Wars? But the young men – she drooped and admitted it – the young men like George looked at you and saw a sofa. Sad, sad, sad!

'Well, I don't know,' George was saying, looking from her to his mother, 'I don't know that I'm staying much longer,' he said. 'Colonel Cochrane knows that. I just took on the job with him while I was looking round after I got demobbed.'

'He's been offered a job,' Mrs. Porter said.

'A pal of mine in Coventry,' said George. 'A garage. There's prospects.'

'I see,' said Laura.

'There's nothing doing here in Wealding,' he said, staring round in disgust, glancing at the privy, at the old net curtains laid over the currant bushes.

'No cinema nearer than Bridbury, never a dance hardly, m'm,' said Mrs. Porter. 'It does make it difficult for the young folks to settle. Mavis is just the same. She's seen life. I can't seem to settle, Mum, she says.'

Mavis had seen life. Mrs. Porter's smile continued placidly to reveal the blackened ruins. The Polish baby, then, had been no more than a souvenir stone, a brass ashtray, a length of embroidery, slipped into the returning daughter's suitcase as proof that she had made the tour.

'He's been to ever so many places, m'm,' Mrs. Porter was saying. 'India, haven't you, George?'

'Yes,' he said sombrely. 'India.'

The cottage seemed to dwindle. George stalked superbly across a blazing landscape, peacocks screamed, sacred old carp moved lazily beneath the pads of blue lilies in the lead tank. The Porters were all-pervading. They pushed out tentacles to Poland and to India. They gazed hungrily at the Bay of Naples. For centuries their blue English eyes must have been staring over the unwieldy prows of ships towards the still untested, threatening shores.

'What did you think of India?' she asked, turning sociably towards George as though they were side by side, shaking out crisp napkins tortured into the shape of bishops' mitres, at some stupid dinner party.

'Too warm for me,' he said, moving his shoulders uncomfortably at the thought. 'And the flies. And the beggars. No, give me old England every time.'

Feeling somewhat irritated – for George looked like splendid bronze which should have been impervious to heat, to insects, even to pity – she said, 'Well, I'm sorry you can't come. I'll tell Mr. Marshall.'

'Yes,' he said nodding. 'Sorry, but that's how it is. You must go where money is these days.'

'And where the girls is, eh?' cried Mrs. Porter, forgetting her soft, servile hiccup, laughing shrilly.

'Yes,' he said simply, 'where girls is, too.'

A child began to cry indoors. That was little Roy, Mavis's baby, said Mrs. Porter, once more smirking, sliding, respectful. 'Go and get him to show Mrs. Marshall, George,' she said, 'for

49

Mavis isn't fit to be seen. He's a lovely kiddy,' she said to Laura, as George came back carrying the baby. He wore only a vest with his Army trousers, and his muscular sunburnt arms held the little boy with peculiar gentleness. Roy's tears hung on his long lashes, but he settled down happily in George's arms. Out of dark, insanitary, crowded holes like this, thought Laura, often comes the astonishing tenderness of George's sort of man for their young. Stephen and his sort do not know it. Stephen would come back from London and go up and say good night to Victoria in her little blue dressing-gown with the pink rabbit on the pocket. Someone is just crazy about their Daddy, Nannie used to say benignly. Then he ran downstairs, smoothing his hair, calling Laura! Philip Drayton was enormously proud of his two boys at Eton. He talked of them with easy, ironic affection when she lunched with him now and then, the bunch of lilies of the valley always on Laura's plate, Philip looking like a stage K.C. with that touch of iron-grey seeming a dash of artful powder at the temples. Ironic, intelligent love, far preferable, of course – but that peculiar, half-feminine tenderness, no. But quite often, she thought, you see it elsewhere. At the seaside, the sallow clerk parading along the wrinkled sands, trousers rolled to the knee of his blue-white legs, a child attached to each hand. He stooped patiently, dabbing their toes in the small waves. When the little girl whispered, he took her behind a rock, unbuttoned her little rubber drawers, and held her out over a sea anemone. Impossible to imagine Stephen or Philip or Colonel Cochrane, that charming old man, holding out their young over a sea anemone.

She looked at George, unselfconsciously nursing his small nephew who had brought Poland into this English Tudor hovel, and thought, Yes, he will go. I see it all. He will leave Wealding, following his fortune to the city. Like a gypsy gazing in a crystal, she saw him prospering, building a home, nursing his own babies. All the Georges will leave Wealding, and what will be left? Old Voller, sucking a pipe in the chimney corner, Roy, the baby, still content to play in the sun.

'What a darling,' she said, touching the child's cheek.

'He's a proper rogue,' said Mrs. Porter proudly. 'Mavis do have a time with him.'

Mavis, a young Mrs. Porter, buttoned with such obvious insecurity during the war into the W.A.A.F. uniform, good natured, easily laughing, always ready for a slap and a giggle – the crystal revealed only too clearly where she was going, too. She would leave Roy here with the other Porter broodlings, and off she would skip, spry as a young cat, returning now and then to dump another kitten in the straw before making off again. The Porters were the adventurers. Without moving from Wealding, Mrs. Porter would sow blue eyes and fair skin over the earth. Beautiful skin, thought Laura, touching Roy's cheek, soft as damask, stained with such pure dazzling colour. He had no father and his mother was spry and shiftless as a young cat, but he had a round and noble head, he was beautiful beneath the Porter dinginess.

'I must go,' said Laura suddenly. 'Goodbye, Mrs. Porter. Goodbye and good luck if I don't see you again,' she said to George.

'Cheerio,' he said, indifferently and amiably gazing at this pleasant sofa, this nice piece of female furniture which had showed up at his back door. He turned, shoving the door open with his shoulder. Roy began to yell again, and Mavis's voice cried, 'Come to Mammy, then!' Laura had a glimpse of them round a slatternly table, little Porter heads rising in height, Mavis with a bristling crest of curlers, a dog's bushy white tail waving, white things airing at the fire, the huge red tin horn of an old-fashioned gramophone yawning out of the darkness like a fabulous sea monster rearing up to suck down the ship and its crew. They were gay, they would like a bit of music in the evenings. Where did they all roost at night? All together, as in a medieval household? Something hot, rank, suffocating seemed to fan out at Laura as the door swung behind George. They were overpowering. Music came over the deserts of the air to them when they turned a knob, they could go into Bridbury and view the celebrated smiles, teeth, bosoms of film stars who were thousands of miles away, but if Mrs. Porter disliked anyone, she might make a little wax figure and stick pins in its stomach. Had the fat corporal Tuck felt no inexplicable twinges, no sudden, sharp, stabbing pains, as he sat in the new local with his arm round some other waist?

'Good-bye!' cried Laura, fleeing.

'If I should hear of anyone wanting a bit of gardening, I'll send a message, m'm,' called Mrs. Porter, nodding easily towards the Prouts' cottage, tacked on next door. She went in and closed the door. Retreating between the lilies, Laura heard their laughter.

VIII

She closed the gate. Mrs. Prout's bicycle leant against a trellis of honeysuckle; she was home from Laura's house. Laura saw her peeping over the sweet geraniums in the window, suspicious, not good cousins with that light piece of goods next door, resentful of Mrs. Marshall trying to have any truck with them. No good will come of it, signalled Mrs. Prout's nose above the sweet geraniums. It would be politic not to notice. The gate clicked into place.

See-saw, said the clock. In a quarter of an hour she had launched Mrs. Porter with a Neapolitan lover on the bright bay, made George's fortune, sent Mavis sliding to meet her light destiny. She laughed at herself. Being much alone encouraged such fancies. As though the See-saw! had released him like a carved wooden figure from a weather-house, Mr. Vyner shot from the church porch, saw her, and waved a hand.

'Hallo, hallo!' he called.

He ran down the steps and crossed the road, lowering his voice as he said, 'You've been visiting my bad patch, I see. Who was it, Prouts or Porters? The Porters?' He shook his head, smiled, and sighed. 'Young George is leaving, his sister told me.

I'm sorry. We could do with more of him in Wealding. But they really are – they *really* are –'

He made a vague, helpless gesture, he laughed helplessly, looking towards the Porters' hump-backed roof as though they overpowered him even at that distance. The Vicar, thought Laura, the traditional butt of kindly comedy, the chevalier of spinsters, crowned with the wilting cucumber sandwiches of a thousand garden parties. And it was Mr. Vyner's fate to look and sound the part of the fruity-voiced churchman, the hearty curer of souls, destined to lose his trousers before the curtain fell on the second act of the roaring farce. He boomed and brayed through the village. He had served in India for many years as an Army chaplain, and he made religion sound like a sort of church parade, with God as the C.O. counting the boots as they clumped in. But he was really good, a saint who had the misfortune to sound like a bore. Laura liked him immensely. He sweated from one end of the village to the other, no distance too long, no hour too late to bring comfort to one of the poor human souls over whom he yearned with such compassion. But the times were out of joint, the healing virtue had gone from his cloth. They did not need him. They did not hold, quoth Mrs. Prout, wrapping her arms in her apron, they did not believe, they did not have any truck with. The grapes in the vineyard had grown thorns to defend themselves against the labourer. Was he sometimes despairing, the weatherman in his ancient house, in the powers of which few fully believed any longer? Difficult to tell, with his high varnished colour, his jolly smile.

'I was trying to get George along to help in the garden,' she said. 'I hadn't heard that he was going.'

'Yes, they're all going,' he said. 'They can't stick it here – not enough doing for them. German prisoners at all the farms – I suppose you've seen them? Splendid workers, Mr. Watson was telling me.' He looked up at the sky. 'Really hot to-day. We've got old Mrs. Pallett's funeral this afternoon.'

He sounded reflective, like old Voller blinking at the clouds and piping through the ghostly keyhole that it was about right to plant the broad beans. This afternoon he would plant old Mrs. Pallett, sow her in the broad patch of Palletts and Prouts and Vollers already twined with the dark roots of the junipers and Scotch briars.

'Good-bye,' he called, turning in at the wicket gate in the high hedge, while Laura walked on with her basket. Over the tall collar of glistening holly, the top storey of the Vicarage loomed like the domed head of a monstrous, costly white elephant tethered in the Vyner garden. It had a magnolia and a tulip tree that were two of Wealding's glories. Into the stable yard at the back, Mr. Vyner would emerge from the door beneath the magnolia and stand putting on his bicycle clips. The loose boxes were useful for storing Mrs. Vyner's chicken food, an old wicker spinal carriage, some wooden frames on which black material had been tacked across the great expansive windows in the war. How sadly, thought Laura, odours of Mrs. Vyner's frozen-cod pie clung to the rep curtains which should have shut out the night on porty stuffiness and spilled candlelight. Sadly, distractedly, Mrs. Vyner shed her light as mother of the parish, with the air of a virgin crushed and trampled by the white elephant, over whose immense carcass she and her husband and two children, their chintzes and bookshelves and jolly university groups showing Mr. Vyner as a rowing man, skated like fleas. She will be there now to meet him, thought Laura, popping out of one of the high draughty rooms in her hair-net. She was exactly the same age as Laura. So Laura had discovered one day, with a sense of shock. Can it be that I, too? she would ask herself incredulously in church, peeping across the aisle at Mrs. Vyner's thin silhouette, beetle dark against the white chrysanthemums of Christmas, the pagan scarlet dahlias, wicked as sin, and the bland yellow marrows of Harvest Festival.

Yes, it can be, thought Laura in the lane, suddenly depressed at the thought of George Porter's blue eyes coolly surveying a nice sofa. Stephen told the kind, the dependable, lies, saying, No more than thirty, saying this and that, but it can be. Mrs. Vyner and I together, a couple of sofas. But girlishness could descend on Mrs. Vyner at the piano, playing a Bach chorale. Then her face became at peace, while her fingers arranged the pattern of exquisite logic, of utter reasonableness, fitting in piece after piece like drawers of a perfect little Chinese box, sliding them in quietly, returning to open one again and show the design, after all a little different, and then closing the doors on the completed thing, and sitting flushed, for a moment translated. Thus should life be, said Mrs. Vyner at her piano. Thus should it be, she would say, with the thorns of the Women's Institute for the moment lifted from her brow, no chick or child clamouring round her feet, and her light grey eyes shining. Both she and Mr. Vyner were musical. He sang, she played, at village concerts, but altogether too highbrow for Wealding, recklessly flinging fugues before swine, old French songs before Mrs. Prout who liked to tap her foot, nod and wink to the rhythm of a good rousing nonny-ho. Sometimes Miss Sewell lugged her 'cello from Church Cottage across the way, old Colonel Cochrane tucked his fiddle under the red dried flap of his chin, and they would have 'a little music,' followed by coffee and cakes over which Stephen would try to look politely incredulous when Mrs. Vyner babbled happily, still translated, that they 'only took a couple of ounces of fat.' But, thought Laura, he liked the music really better than she did. He sat, he listened, he sighed. It took him somewhere, it translated him, too, while her mind, noting Mrs. Vyner blissfully opening drawer after drawer of her perfect little box until the final answer was reached, would slide off wantonly, thinking of the hens (had they shut them up?), of Victoria (was Mrs. Prout getting bored, creaking and telling her fortune with a pack of old cards as she sat on guard in the kitchen?), of the cake she had spoiled that afternoon, of the Indian birds and monkeys swarming in the carved screen which advertised how far the Church Muscular carries the lighted torch. Or, dreadful humiliation, she would feel sleep coming on, so that the edges of her consciousness blurred and ran over like unset jelly, Stephen's profile blurred and wobbled into the shining, shivering edge of one of Mr. Vyner's miniature silver cups won for high jump, the piano seemed to rear up and yawn, she must not, she must not, until – crash! The final chord would seem to split the heavens, they had found the answer, all of them – Colonel Cochrane taking the fiddle out of the pocket of his Indian-burnt neck, Miss Sewell faintly smiling, Stephen suddenly flashing back in hard outline into his chair. No, she was not musical really, and neither was Victoria, frisking, poor little sacrificial lamb, with her leather music case jigging in her hand towards Bridbury and half an hour with Miss Trasker over 'Little Gavotte' and 'Water Lily Elves.' But as they all sat there, leaning slightly forward, with that floating, translated look, she would see them and the room with sudden clarity as though they were a bright mosaic picture held in the rounded crystal of their music. The shabby rep curtains shut out the world on this small circle of dedicated effort. Thus and thus should life be, stated the 'cello sonorously. Reason, order, and logic, said Mrs. Vyner's piano. The room seemed to swim in the crystal, secret and isolated, like the meeting-place of an early Christian community, singing in defiance of the pagan darkness outside. Or so it would appear to Laura in the split second of extra clarity before her chin went down in a vast, an entirely shameful nod . . .

How hot it was! The midday heat was rising to a head, like milk to the boil, singing in a clotted hum of bees, of crickets among the sorrel and daisies, of gnats dancing above the cresses tugged all one way by the trickle of water running under the hedge. An old woman came out with a pail, hobbling across the lane to the tap dripping among the moss. She had lived to see men flying overhead like birds; to stand among the hollyhocks watching bombs spluttering across the stars to kill a family forty miles away; to turn a switch and hear the great voice from Westminster correcting her kitchen clock. All the same, she had to hobble with a pail to the tap among the mosses and the green viper tongues of ferns. At night large shadows would set oil lamps above the potted geraniums in the tiny windows. The cottage gardens were bright pocket handkerchiefs embroidered with rice-paper crinkled poppy, peppery lupin, stout rose, and Canterbury bell. But the hedges, closing their shade over Laura's sticky shoulders, were nearly as bright, hanging out dog-rose and honeysuckle, spreading purple vetch, fine as ladies' hair, and ragged robin, cut like medieval sleeve edges, and frosted lilac orchis between the totter grass. I love you, Lulu, a wood-pigeon went on repeating, deep in the woods, ending with a sudden abrupt Yes! What a lovely day, my poor Stephen, thought Laura. Yes, at last a really perfect summer day.

And she turned thankfully in at her own front gate. The house was closed, each window carefully shut before leaving by Mrs. Prout, to whom Wealding was full of threatening characters with an eye to Mrs. Marshall's tarnished silver. I am not at home, said the house coldly with blank eyes and pursed lips. I am a desirable residence no longer desirable, for Chandler is dead, and the bindweed drowns the Mermaid rose in green tendrils. Ethel and Violet have gone. Ring my bell, madam, and you will no longer hear them trip across the parquet, or draw in, from beyond their trim shoulders, my exhalation of a freshly polished, loved and cherished house . . . Those tiles, Laura was thinking as she felt in her purse for her key, must really be seen to, or we'll get a flood in the next heavy rains. She went round to the kitchen door and let herself in. Silence of an empty house just ticking over with the faint arterial life of a coal dropping in the grate, a pipe sizzling, a chair creaking as though some ghost had quitted it. A whiff of Mrs. Prout, compounded of sweat and flowered cotton and peppermint drops. The cat sat with her feet exactly together, coldly unwelcoming. Stuffy had not returned.

She had just put her basket on the table when the telephone bell shrilled through the closed rooms.

IX

When Laura came back from speaking to her mother, there were immediately a great many things to do. She unpacked the packages she had bought in Bridbury, thinking, as she picked sodden bits of the *Times* leader off wet fish skin, How horribly dead food is, how much deader than one ever suspected when it turned up by magic, nicely browned with crescents of lemon, waiting above little lamps on the sideboard. 'Mr. Molotov' – she picked him off the fish scales – 'the position in Trieste to-day must –' and with a gesture of irritation she whipped the position in Trieste away from the damp mournful slab which had surely never swum and sported among sunlit rocks and weeds. The position in Bridbury to-day had been a shortage of fish, so that Mr. Kellett, the fishmonger, was in a bad temper with the long line of waiting women, slapping the grey neutral slabs into their baskets, or, to the favoured few, offering more recognizably maritime creatures with ugly flat heads and accusing goggle eyes. It's terrible, Mr. Kellett had grumbled, diving his scarlet hands into a bucket of goggling monsters, it's never been worse, not even in the war, it hasn't. The line of women had swayed and sighed, murmuring uneasily, staring with depression at the dwindling pile of fish, summoning up a false brightness when their turn came to step forward under Mr. Kellett's angry little blue eyes. And to-night, chewing the dead slab which she would disguise as something or other, Stephen would say thoughtfully that it was odd what had happened to the soles. Had they disappeared from the seas, a war-time casualty? Not that this was not, of course, perfectly delicious, he would add kindly . . .

She moved round the larder and pantry opening lids, taking down jars, stowing away Rosemary's seed cake, Stuffy's biscuits, the oranges which had crowned the morning's expedition. Mrs. Prout had washed the lettuce and left Laura's lunch tray set on the side, its silver and glass and neat napkin seeming to say, with a toss of Mrs. Prout's head, What's the odds? Let the poor creature eat her bit of rabbit's food in the style to which she has been accustomed. No body in it, Mrs. Prout would sniff over the wet lettuce, but let her pretend to have a real meal with all the refinements of side plate and folded damask and glass goblet (one of the four survivors). But first, thought Laura, she would start some of the evening's cooking before eating. She began to move pans back and forth off the stove. She used the colander, the grater, wooden spoons of various sizes, and a small army of basins. Her cheeks became flushed. Would the sauce bind? And lo, it bound, while her heart did likewise. But with a hiss, something else boiled over disastrously, so that the cat, who knew Laura, got up and withdrew in prudent haste. A sad brown smell invaded the cluttered kitchen. Mopping up the ruins, Laura thought of Mrs. Abbey, their former and best cook, Mrs. Abbey, who had been killed by a flying bomb while taking a cup of tea with her niece Flo in Putney. Mrs. Abbey's kitchen, while dinner was brewing, had been marvellously neat, on the stove the saucepans boiling peacefully, on the enamel table top under the clinical light the egged and breaded fillets of sole lying waiting in a row. Laura remembered coming in to the kitchen one autumn morning (Chandler had brought in a basket of pale-yellow pears, Victoria's cheeks were red as her little coat as she sat in her pram, the spiders' webs had looped sparkling bridges across the smoky blue ravines of the Michaelmas daisies). There stood Mrs. Abbey, making an apple charlotte, Laura remembered perfectly. Her hands flew, trimming bread crusts, lining the dish, adding fruit and cloves and brown sugar which immediately looked good, appetizing, when her fat pink hands touched them. Laura had stopped there watching, for the operation had the fascination of the simple thing swiftly and perfectly done. Poor Mrs. Abbey, who lived only for her cooking and the Royal Family (with an especial weakness for the Duchess of Kent – she had a whole album pasted up with the Greek profile and the sad, crooked smile), she had long left the Marshalls when she met her end, when out of the silence the walls caved in with a sickening roar on her narrow dedicated life, on her podgy pink hand lifting to her lips the cup of tea with Flo. And now Laura, in Mrs. Abbey's unrecognizable kitchen, went through the same gestures of trimming bread crusts, draining, chopping, but with the slowness and slight stiffness of the performing poodle who had learnt the routine too late in life. Phew! She straightened up from the stove, pushing the curly hair away from her forehead. It was hot, terribly hot in the kitchen. She wanted a drink of water. And now she would carry the tray into the garden and eat her salad.

The lawn was thickly powdered with daisies, over which Stephen swore hopelessly in the evenings when he dragged the lawn mower out of the potting-shed. Laura thought them prettier than the bare patches of burnt leaves which followed his over-heavy-handed sprinkling of lawn sand, for Stephen was another performing poodle, struggling clumsily through the routine of the departed Chandler. Between him and old Voller, most things were too late or too early, frost took them, mice ate them, unknown blights descended. In the week-ends Stephen struggled frantically with the garden, which turned a sour face and mourned for Chandler. But the flower borders still, with dogged herbaceous loyalty, pushed up spires of rose and yellow, patches of blue and velvet maroon with dark eyes from which, as jauntily pretty as they, the wild convolvulus hung its white trumpet and the thistle thrust a purple rosette four steely feet into the air. The bees bumbled about in it contentedly, the cat scratched delicately and unreproved beneath the branching lupins. Now, as Laura sat eating her salad in the shade, it seemed to shimmer in a haze of heat and insect humming and scraping. The syringa, which had been a cloud of frozen air in the early morning light, hung white and gold in the sun's warmth, lolling, showering scent and golden powder from its open bosom. On a cluster of pinks a butterfly like a tiger-lily petal settled, fanned itself, staggered off drunk with summer. And a beautiful beetle, edged with turquoise round its head and with purple round its pear-shaped body of jet armour, struggled wildly through the daisies near Laura's feet.

Watching the beetle blunder through the forests, hastening on in its unending pilgrimage over the earth, Laura remembered with slight depression that her mother was coming to stay. She would tell Stephen to-night over dinner, and he would say instantly, Oh, splendid! Then a careful pause. How long is she coming for? he would ask casually. Only a week, she would be able to say reassuringly. Just while she sees Briggs.

'Such a nuisance, darling,' Mrs. Herriot had mourned on the telephone, delicate and clear over the air from Cornwall. 'I broke a tooth, and I'll have to see Briggs about it.'

She rang up always at the expensive time of day, which annoyed Stephen's sense of order. Not that he was mean, but reasonable people waited until evening for long-distance calls, when the line was clearer and the charge less dear. Mrs. Herriot, however, would ring up immediately she wanted to say something, to ask for the address of a watch repairer, to ask Laura if she had seen in *The Times* the death of that charming Major Phipps-Lumley – did she remember the Phipps-Lumleys all those years ago at Cadenabbia? They had always made a point of sending Christmas cards even through the war, and now there he was, dead suddenly at Tunbridge Wells, and Laura should certainly write. Not a thought did Mrs. Herriot give, Stephen would remark irritably, to dwindling income and staggering telephone bill which the poor old devil, his father-in-law, would have to foot. In her clear, imperious voice she would give a number half-way across England, as though the dumb black instrument were a genie that it fascinated her to call out of the bottle, just another slave to summon with a clap of her hands. Laura, unfortunately, had the same incorrigible family weakness.

'If you could have me, say, next week,' Mrs. Herriot had said, 'I would ring up Briggs and get the secretary to make appointments for me right away. He's frightfully booked up, but I know he'll fit me in for an emergency. And it's much more pleasant staying with you, darling, than in London which is so stuffy and depressing too, nowadays.'

Mr. Briggs of Wimpole Street – for years the Herriots had gone to him. Surely, Stephen would say, there must be excellent dentists in Truro, for instance, without your mother trailing all the way to London for that sort of thing? But in certain things Mrs. Herriot was inflexible, following, like a mesmerized hen, a chalk line of behaviour which the years had laid down. One went to Briggs for teeth, to the Army and Navy Stores for wine, to Woolland's for hats, to a guild of distressed invalid gentle-women in Kensington for underclothes, to *The Times* Book Club for the latest biography. Right through the war Mrs. Herriot had come up from Cornwall on her little foraging expeditions, not bothering about the blitzes, as indomitable as Mr. Briggs himself who, when not so distant crashes shook the windows of his consulting-room, would simply select another instrument and say, One really can't notice this sort of thing, can one? The lip a *leetle* more relaxed, if you please.

'What about Daddy?' Laura had asked on the telephone, and Mrs. Herriot had replied, Aunt Vi would come and see to him for the week.

Dependable Aunt Vi, thought Laura, the indispensable female relative always ready to hand, always bright though without more than a church-mouse pittance, herself a distressed gentlewoman though not making French knots on Mrs. Herriot's nightgowns in Kensington. She was another slave whom Mrs. Herriot summoned relentlessly from the bottle with a clap of her fine hands. Oh, these Anglo-Indian women, Stephen would all too obviously think as he glanced at his mother-in-law's faded governing profile in the candlelight. Mrs. Herriot used Aunt Vi quite remorselessly, calling her from her room in a private hotel in Bayswater only when there was work afoot – a domestic crisis, or a village shindig involving bran tubs and endless bread-and-butter cutting, or Arthur to be minis-tered to while his wife headed for Wimpole Street. Colonel Herriot could not be left unattended. All his life he had been looked after, for years he had barely put on his own boots, and if he were alone for even a few days he visibly wilted, became mournful and bloodshot as an old spaniel padding round the house. Aunt Vi, turning up staunchly from Bayswater, would supply the necessary female figure to sit behind the coffee-pot at breakfast, to say Change your socks, Arthur, when he came in wet from gardening, to offer suggestions after dinner as he groaned over *The Times* crossword puzzle, sitting in the chintz armchair near the gruesomely dashing photograph of himself as a young cavalry officer.

'Poor old Aunt Vi,' Laura had said, suddenly smitten with compunction at the thought of the slight moustache, the cheerful meekness (she never failed to remember Victoria's birthday, accompanying the little gift with a pretty card of bunnies or kitties inscribed in elegant writing 'From your old Auntie Vi'). 'How is she, Mother?'

'Oh, Vi's always strong as a horse,' Mrs. Herriot had replied, with the slight touch of annoyance which followed attention diverted from herself. Her voice became softer. 'How are *you*, childie? Stephen isn't letting you do too much as usual, I hope?'

'No, oh no,' Laura had said brightly and hypocritically.

'And my Victoria? Give her a hug from me, and tell her –' and the conversation tailed off in grandmotherly endearments, a few afterthoughts, and a storm of time signals going off like Chinese crackers. 'Goodbye until Tuesday, then, darling,' Mrs. Herriot had said. Laura, hanging up, had pictured her mother doing the same thing at home, waiting for a moment, in the hall where the telephone stood on an Ashanti stool beneath crossed assegais and a miniature of a military ancestor. Through the open door, the garden would be humming with heat and colour as Laura's garden hummed. Mrs. Herriot would remain gazing out for a moment at the queer tropical spikes of the yucca, the little stone figure of an Indian god with his fingers chipped off by one of the evacuees who had been with the Herriots during the war. For a brief interval, Laura guessed, her mother would be still, marshalling her forces, staring with faded blue eyes into the sunshine, before she picked up the receiver again, and, giving the London number as slowly and crisply as though the St. Pol post office spoke nothing but Hindustani, set about summoning from the air the soothing genie of Mr. Briggs.

(The beetle had overturned on a plantain root and had a few moments of humiliating misery, working its legs and blue-black overlapping plates, before Laura moved it over with a blade of grass and it hastened away. She finished her salad and sat on, thinking about her mother and father.)

When she took Victoria down for a little visit, it was like going back to another world, seen through the nostalgic lens of world catastrophe. Nothing has altered here, said her parents' home. Everything was exactly as she remembered it – the chintzes covered with bunches of violets; the silver photograph frames enshrining women friends in Court feathers and men friends in Levée splendour; the water-colours of Kashmir; the heads of beautiful horned animals sprouting from little wooden shields in the dining-room; the Herriot coat of arms on frail china cups in musty cabinets; the white painted furniture in Mrs. Herriot's bedroom; the rose geranium salts beside the huge, coffin-like, mahogany framed bath; the leopard skin in Colonel Herriot's little study; the regimental groups of men with heavy drooping moustaches; the Army chests in the top passage; the hideous cloisonné jug brought back by some relative from the Boxer looting; the swords and native weapons on the staircase; the mounted elephant's foot on the desk; the polo sticks in the stand with the umbrellas; the biscuit-tin beside the bed in the guest room; the faded photograph in the lavatory of Colonel Herriot with Mrs. Herriot and a native bearer, outside their tent looking at a dead roebuck. The British Empire seemed to have contracted into the modest white house through which the same old friends came and went on quiet visits – General

Sands, Colonel Potts, Major Tooms, a little more shrivelled and dusty-skinned than Laura remembered in her girlhood, though their eyes were bright with the rejuvenation of watching on draughty hilltops all those years for an enemy who never came. Everything was exactly as Laura remembered it in the house, with the museum-like effect of a room kept just so for a dead son who would never come back. Bewilderment curdled the bright blue of her father's eyes as he rustled through *The Times*, appealing to someone to tell him what They were up to – They meaning the Labour Government, the Russians, the proletariat, the whole palpably insane and suicidal universe. Round him, for the moment, his little private world remained standing, for it had been soundly constructed of good things designed to last many lifetimes. The solidity of teak and mahogany denied the world's quaking foundations, the silver photograph frames were more real than the yellowing Edwardian features they enclosed. Only the heads of the beautiful, agile, horned creatures moulted slightly and mournfully. General Sands and Colonel Herriot, who had shot in India together, walked stiffly back and forth on the gravel path outside the dining-room window, two old men discussing what They were up to, while the yellow glass eyes of the heads watched them, it seemed, somewhat ironically. Her father, Laura had noticed particularly on that last visit, was looking very old, and her heart had ached with love and sadness.

(She got up and carried her tray indoors. She washed up, fed the cat, and got a bowl for the gooseberries. And out she went again, snatching up an old hat, for it would be grilling sitting there among the spiny bushes.)

Her mother, she thought, had not adapted to things. The war had flowed past her like a dark, strong river, never pulling her into its currents, simply washing to her feet the minor

68

debris of evacuees who broke the statue's fingers and spoiled a mattress, of food shortages, or worry over Laura who was close to bombs, and worked too hard, and had tragically lost her fresh looks. Now, said Mrs. Herriot, thank God it was over, and everything could get back to normal again. She brushed her hands together and looked round commandingly. Mr. Briggs and the Army and Navy Stores had survived, the distressed gentlewomen had crawled out of the basements and were executing French knots and hand-faggoting again from their couches of pain. Now, darling, said Mrs. Herriot, the servants will be coming back, they will be glad to get out of those awful uniforms, out of those appalling huts into a decent house with hot baths and a nice bed. And when they did not, she simply could not understand it. Down in St. Pol, the girls had not yet caught on to the new ideas. Mrs. Herriot swooped down occasionally like an eagle on the depressing slate-roofed cottages and carried off another fourteen-year-old child, raw but willing, who would learn to cram her red wrists through neat white cuffs and to bring in the Colonel's grog-tray every evening. So the mahogany continued to reflect the silver polo cups pleasantly, the Herriot world held together for a little longer in its deadness of glacial chintz strewn with violets and side tables strewn with the drooping moustached faces of yesteryear. The war had been horrible, really ghastly – had not the Carruthers lost three nephews, the Whyte-Jevons two airmen sons and a daughter drowned in a torpedoed ship, Colonel Herriot's niece Betty her husband in a Jap prison camp? But mercifully it was over, said Mrs. Herriot, and Laura must really pay attention to her appearance a little more now that Stephen was home.

(There hung the gooseberries, fat greyish-green lanterns and smaller red ones, hairy as a man's chest. Laura sat down on the ground with the bowl in her lap and began to pick. The heat, rising to its midday head, seemed to have throbbed and spilled over, or else it was the shade of the fruit bushes, for it was pleasant sitting here. She reached for a bough of large gooseberries, and the bough spitefully jabbed its long thorns into her hand.)

Your hands, Laura darling! They used to be so pretty, quite one of your best features, Mrs. Herriot would cry out in horror. Hands are such a give-away, she often said complacently in the old days, surveying her own well-shaped fingers. When she came to stay with Laura, she sat looking round, on her charming crumpled face the ghost of a sniff more subtle and disparaging than any of Mrs. Prout's. The disparagement, Laura irritably knew, was all directed against Stephen. Colonel Herriot had been looked after all his life, he had to be constantly coaxed, and stayed with the female comforts of Aunt Vi behind the coffee-tray, the little maid to bring his shaving-water and his grog-tray, but his wife still kept up the pleasing fiction that the male was the protector.

'Stephen should see that it's too much for you,' she said to Laura. 'It worries me to death thinking of you struggling along here with the housework and cooking and the child. Victoria had an enormous split in her blazer yesterday – had you noticed it? She said it had been like that for weeks. My darling, you're looking dreadfully fagged out. During the war of course it was necessary, but now Stephen must absolutely insist –'

The ghost of Mrs. Herriot's delicate sniff would haunt Laura for the week that she was in their home. It would gently vibrate the cobweb which Mrs. Prout's broom always by-passed on the picture rail, it would ruffle the dish water in which Laura was guiltily washing up, it would pursue Laura and Stephen into their beds. Sitting knitting a jersey for Victoria (the indignant speed of her needles seemed to envisage a granddaughter naked as well as unkempt), her back very straight, her horn-rimmed glasses on her pretty pinched nose, Mrs. Herriot had said on the occasion of the last sortie to Briggs:

'After all, Laura, here you are, only thirty-six –'

'Thirty-eight.'

'Thirty-eight, then.' Carefully controlled annoyance for a moment passed over Mrs. Herriot's face. 'Quite young enough, at all events, to be enjoying yourself more than you do. So far as I can see, you spend the entire day doing the work of an unpaid domestic servant. When I think how you were brought up –'

She made a sweeping gesture with a knitting-needle. In the arc of the movement, she seemed to be contemplating for a reproachful moment the tennis parties, the little trips to Italy, the hunt balls. Laura had never learnt how to dust a room in her life. Though the Herriots were only modestly well off, they managed to get value for their money, living quietly down at St. Pol, and people liked Laura, asked her to stay, mounted her on their horses. At a hunt ball she had met Stephen Marshall, staying with friends in the neighbourhood. A young man called Marshall from London, 'something in the City' – Mrs. Herriot had disliked the sound of it from the very beginning. Her needles clicked in and out of the blue jersey for Stephen's daughter. She looked absently at the photograph of Laura in her wedding dress, a tall girl in a mist of tulle and Grandmother Herriot's old Limerick.

'Such a lovely dress,' she said. She sighed. 'By the way, how is Philip? Doing very well, so I heard from someone the other day – who was it? Oh, his aunt, of course, old Miss Crompton. Still so wonderful, after having had soldiers in her house all through the war and dozens of evacuees and heavens knows what.' She counted stitches. She sat bolt upright, her feet in the worn brocade slippers close together as a cat's. Philip Drayton, her silence said louder than words, would know how to look after his wife. If you had married him, as I wanted you to do, you would not be slaving away here with your hands spoilt and your hair grey. Disappointment and strong Indian light had creased the skin round her eyes and mouth with a multitude of fine lines like old tissue paper. She looked up at Laura pathetically.

'Thirty-eight,' she said. 'I can't believe that you're thirty-eight, darling. How this frightful war has eaten up everything.'

Daughters ran away, away. One doesn't really know what's going on, her eyes had said pathetically. Laura kissed her. She straightened her glasses, and the crisp governing note came back into her voice.

'That charwoman of yours, darling,' she said. 'That Mrs. Prout, isn't it? Does she never say "madam"?'

(Laura's bowl was half-full, but she seemed to have made very little impression on the forest of greyish-green lanterns. The garden had been planted in the cheerful belief that there would always be plenty of hands to net, to pick, to bottle, and make jam. Beyond the lichen-grey forest of gooseberries hung the currants, white and red, fabulous Oriental clusters shining among their leaves as though dipped in spring water. The jays screamed and bounced over the raspberry canes, and a black-bird landed beside Laura, cocked his head and punctured a hairy red berry before he noticed her and fled with a startled 'Mink!' Laura's left foot had gone to sleep. She shifted her position.)

Once or twice a year Philip asked her out to lunch, a pleasant reunion, comfortably padded by two successful marriages. How's Stephen? Fine, thanks. And Cicely? Cicely's wonderful. The boys, too. Have I told you about Hugh –? And he would tell a little anecdote about the boys, affectionate, sardonic, for he adored them, but had never in his life held them with the womanish tenderness with which George Porter had held the illegitimate son of his sister Mavis. The head waiter, hovering, asked, Everything all right, Mr. Drayton? He was the kind of man to whom head waiters attached themselves instinctively, like sucker fish to a whale. The stigmata of success had been visible even to Mrs. Herriot fifteen years ago. The world's mess had by-passed the Draytons, merely setting a higher value, in its desperate need, on brains such as Philip's. He was going into politics, Mrs. Herriot had heard from old Miss Crompton. Cicely would be an immense help to him, and their house in Westminster had not even lost a window in the blitzes, they had a treasure of an old family cook and an older family parlourmaid, who called him Mr. Philip and did not know that the age of the Common Man had arrived. He felt guilty about their luck, he said last time he and Laura lunched together, for most of their friends were existing in appalling discomfort. His aunt, old Miss Crompton, had shut up a wing, the Bampings were selling Rysdale. With charming tact he averted his eyes from Laura's hands, which he used to admire.

My son-in-law, Philip Drayton – how handsomely he would have beaked out of one of the silver photograph frames among the bunches of slippery violets at home. Her father would have liked it too. And how nearly it had happened only Laura and Philip knew, though he had never been able to understand why the coin had come down with Stephen's head uppermost. Even now, after all these years, he looked at her speculatively. He wondered. Why? Because of a look, she wanted to tell him, though he would not believe her. A look and a tone of voice, and suddenly the heavens had opened and a stern angel cried, Thou shalt not! It was winter and Philip had come down to stay with his aunt. Everyone smiled when they saw her and Philip together, and Major Tooms, who was visiting the Herriots, had stroked his little grey moustache with a bony iodine-yellow finger, looked at her as though musing something doggish, and suddenly asked Mrs. Herriot what had happened to that devilish handsome girl Grace Something-or-other, who had been staying with them in India at the time of the Delhi Durbar. The house seemed full of a kind of rosy gas composed of countless naked *amorini*, pushing Laura and Philip gently together, unveiling each new day disguised as the little maid of the moment when she clumped in with the hot-water can, quenched it in the blue felt cosy, and whispered, Good morning, Miss Laura. Her father was very tender with her, her mother chattered constantly on the telephone. She had two new dresses, a white lace, and a water-green tulle with butterflies lighting on the shoulder straps and drifting over the skirt. She remembered the green dress particularly, for she loved it. And suddenly the *amorini* had nudged her and Philip out for a walk together one late afternoon when the sun was hanging, a dark-red ball, in a sky which seemed hazed with bonfire smoke. The air was peppermint cold in the nostrils, birds sat looking rumpled and dismayed on the bare boughs, there was a bitter earthy smell in the woods as though the lees of the year had been stirred and left to settle under a scum of withered bryony in the ditches. They came to a lake, frozen among the reeds, the track of webbed feet writing Chinese characters over the powdered ice. 'Let's have a slide,' said Laura, laughing, running and bringing her feet together. It was quite shallow there, and her leg was only wet to the ankle, but Philip made a great fuss. 'Didn't you hear it crack?' he asked. 'I was just too late to shout and warn you. Now we'd better get you home as quickly as possible. Do you feel cold, Laura? Your stocking is soaking, you idiotic child.' She did not feel cold and told him so cheerfully, but he rushed her home with a look which swathed her protectively in blankets. 'Go straight up and change,' he said with quiet authority in the hall. 'Better still, have a good hot bath, my dear. I'm not going to have you take any risks with yourself.' She looked down at him from the staircase. The electric light was already on, the afternoon was fading in the quick winter dusk, and she saw her lover with great distinctness against the background of assegais and a large native hat of soft coloured straw which had been brought back by some Herriot from abroad. Philip's expression struck her suddenly as quite insufferable. He was extremely good-looking in the narrow, fine-boned legal way which looked impressive in a wig. Complacency sat upon him so that the corners of his full mouth seemed to emit a little bubble of self-satisfaction, a tiny emanation of some deep inward congratulation. Dear Laura, said his look as he stood in the Herriots' hall, always so vague and scatterbrained, but we will be able to change all that. His look stamped her as though she were a parcel, addressed Mrs. Philip Drayton, about which they must now take no risks. He cleared his throat. The bubble beaded at the pitcher's brim. It burst, and his beautifully clear, precise voice rang through the hall like doom. 'If you have any mustard, it would be a good idea to soak your feet,' he said. Warning thunder seemed to sound in Laura's ears, the *amorini* retreated in disorder before the stern angel shouting from the heavens, Thou shalt not! He is a pompous bore, she thought in dismay, a pompous bore. She heard her father beginning to bumble out of his little study at the sound of their voices. He spent most of his afternoons in the depressing little brown snuggery, napping, reading the paper, staring through the tobacco smoke at all the handsome, heavily moustached faces of men now dead, or shrivelled, dusty, like Tooms and Sands. Laura heard the Colonel dropping a pipe, bumping into a chair like a large clumsy dog on his way to the door. She turned and fled wildly up the stairs. The next evening, dancing in the water-green tulle dress, she met Stephen Marshall, a young man from London who was staying with the Trehearnes over at Polruddock as a partner for their third jolly and unmarried daughter Connie.

(And now the bowl was quite full of gooseberries. There was no more room for even one.)

X

Stephen would take them up to London to-morrow to give to Foster and Miss Margesson in his office. Whoppers, eh? he would say proudly, holding a gooseberry between finger and thumb, for he had never outgrown the townsman's pleasure and astonishment at the perpetually recurring miracle of the soil. Besides that, he had cleared the bushes of weeds himself, hoeing all one Sunday. Every berry would seem a victory personally wrested from the devilish bindweed, the groundsel, the ground elder with its patient, endless subterranean tunnelling of white bone. Whoppers, eh? he would say, and Miss Margesson would reply – but there Laura had to leave them. When Stephen kissed her good-bye in the morning and the car wheels crunched on the gravel, he disappeared into a masculine world of which she knew nothing. The City had the strangeness and mystery, never to be explored, of the St. James's Street clubs at which she sometimes peered from a taxi on her occasional visits to London. Seen through the yellowish fog of a winter afternoon, these strongholds would seem to swim in their own rich yellow fog which glinted on pallid bald heads and a corner of tarnished gilt from the frame of, perhaps, some former Viceroy or Prime Minister, on crimson brocade looped with tassels, on an old servant approaching the vast windows to draw curtains, to shut out, to make secure with his embracing ritual gesture this port-winy, sombre, mysterious inner sanctum of England's might. What went on in there, Laura knew no more than she could follow the endless subterranean tunnelling of the ground elder. And Stephen's private world defeated her imagination as completely. She had been brought up among her father's friends whose actions were clear as daylight. They gave orders in quiet voices, saying to one Come! and he cometh, and to another Go! and he goeth. They dispensed justice under topee and punkah, they shot beautiful horned creatures which later, pinned to little wooden shields like butterflies to corks, moulted sadly over the mahogany cellarette. They strode across England in tweeds, or rode in pink, bringing death to everything that winged and ran before them in the crisp autumn mornings. They retired from their power and glory to small villas in which they lived on their pensions, brooding like sad old dogs in tobacco-brown snuggeries among photographic evidence of the past. But business, in the Herriot world, was just faintly suspect, something which crinkled Mrs. Herriot's nose in its delicate spectral sniff. Laura had been taught to feel that too. Understanding about money was as much a give-away for a woman as hands, so she was stupid about money. The Herriots were poor, by comparison with many of their friends, but somehow one went for little holidays to Cadenabbia where one met people like oneself, such as the Phipps-Lumleys, enjoying the advantageous exchange and the good cheap living. Somehow the water-green dance dress fell from heaven, the little maids clumped in with the brass hot-water cans, the Herriot world would last for ever. Only Mrs. Herriot believed that it was still lasting.

So Laura was stupid about money and was completely unable

to imagine how Miss Margesson, embedded somewhere like a drab fly in the clouded substance of Stephen's day, would talk to Stephen. Miss Margesson was marvellous. She had been a wonder all through the war, keeping things together at the office, going every night to the shelter with Mother, an old lady of seventy-five who minded terribly about the bombs. Laura had gone up to London after Stephen cabled her, to see if there was anything she could do for Miss Margesson, who had come up from the shelter one morning to find their home in ruins. Thank you, Mrs. Marshall, Miss Margesson had said in a series of jerky telegraphic formulas, most kind, but nothing really, Mother with my sister in Epsom, naturally shock, staying with a friend in Finchley, most fortunate her daughter's room was free through joining Wrens, but most thoughtful, really most kind. 'Do come down to Wealding, Miss Margesson,' Laura had urged her. 'Come to stay for a week or month, anything you like.' Most kind, Miss Margesson had said, but somehow can't leave it just now. She did not explain whether she meant the office or London, acrid-smelling outside the glassless windows, last night's floating black particles still falling softly as snow, as though the whole of humanity were despairingly burning its papers before giving up, getting out. Laura had felt guilty, waiting for the train to go home to Wealding. It was about four o'clock on a winter afternoon, the faces of the people on the platform were turned expectantly down the line, waiting for the overdue train, and now and then uneasily to the sky, from which came the yawning noise of gunfire. There was the tenseness of approaching dusk, when the drawbridge would be hauled up. Laura had felt dreadfully guilty, thinking of Miss Margesson in Finchley, while she was scuttling back to Wealding where the sirens would wail from Bridbury, the engines would grumble above the moon-torn clouds, but one could think comfortingly of the fields which would take the splintering shock, the hills which would shudder but would not fall on the sleeping child. When the train came in and the people jumped out, shouldering their bundles, and marched resolutely up the platform into the besieged castle, she looked at them almost with love. They plodded forward as though they were keeping an appointment with life, clasping their belongings, taking no notice of the grey sky which kept on with its hollow, inhuman yawning noises. She wanted to cry to them, Get back into the train again! Don't you know what happened last night? And at the same time she was in a panic fever to get out herself, to get home to Victoria, to leave the city with its terrible feeling of suspense and doom.

Well, thank God all that is over, thought Laura, putting the bowl of gooseberries in the larder. Miss Margesson's mother had died in Epsom, comfortably in her bed, not in a bunk surrounded by the snores of strangers. Stephen was back, Miss Margesson and he retreated every day into the inner sanctum where Laura could not follow them. Had a good day, darling? she would ask in the evening, but it was a mere dutiful formula. The submerged seven-eighths of his life belonged to Miss Margesson, who would pop the gooseberries in her case and immediately make them seem mercantile, thought Laura, a nice little dividend which she would prudently bank into bottles in the kitchenette of her bed-sitting-room. Was she lonely there, hanging up the indefinite office garments, sitting down to the something on a tray? Perhaps she even missed the war, which must have assaulted her stiff, shy virginity, forcing her to telegraph out of her isolation to others, to lie down and sleep among strangers. Poor old Margesson, Stephen would say, taking her up some gooseberries, a few eggs. But admirable Margesson, too, she would be able to understand the worries which made Stephen look gloomy sometimes in the evenings when they had finished running about and were at last sitting down together for a few minutes. He would lower his book and sit staring, thinking deeply. It was a give-away to understand about money; she was such a fool that Miss Margesson would regard her with the righteous contempt of an excellent secondary education and a brain which saw things in as precise and logical a pattern as Mrs. Vyner's music, but even she, Laura, knew that a flaw now ran across the foundations of the pretty, comfortable house. Private means, the sugar which had faintly reconciled Mrs. Herriot to swallowing the business pill for her daughter, had lost their comfortable-sounding properties in the public, universal disaster. The Marshalls also had connections with the East. The Herriots had helped to make the map an English pink all over the world, they had sat down in the cool of the morning to dispense justice, accepting the exile which in the end would make England seem an exile. The Marshalls had followed on, shrewdly seeing their advantage in the stifling port and the beautiful wild hill country, so that old Andrew Marshall had sent his sons to Eton, his grandson had bought a family mansion in a Kensington square which had been destroyed by a bomb in 1941, and his great-grandson Stephen Marshall had said My man's good on roses, in the perpetual lazy Sunday afternoon of the thirties. But the jungle had closed over the tea bush and the young rubber plantation as ravenously as the weeds had eaten the roses; the thick black smoke rising from the burning factory and the bombed wharves had made an ironic joke of old Andrew's comfortable nineteenth-century maxim, 'Safe as houses.' Nothing was safe, as Miss Margesson could no doubt prove with damning figures if you gave her half a chance. Some people, said Mr. Kellett, the fishmonger in Bridbury, had done well out of this war and no

81

mistake. Some people come in here with their fur coats who wouldn't have afforded tail of cod before the war, and now screaming for turbot, Mr. Kellett had said to Laura, staring at her with his angry little eyes as though perpetually soured with the anxieties of his trade, the damp slabs, the dipping of the hands in and out of icy water. But Colonel Herriot, bewildered blue eyes on the shrinking globe, demanded to be told what They were up to. Stephen sat in the evening, when it was too dark to garden, thinking, lowering the book on paper and staring gloomily in front of him. The Herriot and the Marshall worlds were now flawed and shrinking.

Somehow, thought Laura as she went through the house, somehow she would have to protect Stephen from the silent, accusing ghost of a sniff which would haunt them for the week of Mrs. Herriot's visit. My poor Stephen, she thought, you shall not be worried, you shall not. It is bad enough that you should have to sit in a hot office on a day like this, working mysteries with Miss Margesson for Victoria and me. A small clock struck in the drawing-room, which wore its Wednesday air of a temple swept and garnished, dedicated to callers and the cucumber sandwich and the cup of tea. Mrs. Prout had plumped the cushions, drawn the chairs in a circle which announced, We are ready, let the company enter. And every now and then, to appease the room, they had a little party. Last week, for instance, the Cochranes and Bill and Honor Farleigh had come to dinner. It was the Cochranes' last visit before they left Wealding. They were going to live in Ireland, and a good deal of the conversation was taken up with their new house. You could live like a fighting cock there, said Colonel Cochrane, you could buy a Georgian house with a decent bit of shooting for a reasonable price, as he had done, and get any amount of Irish girls out of the bog to come as maids and be glad of the chance. He was tall and grizzled; kind Mrs. Cochrane was soft and round.

'I've had enough of England,' he said. 'You'd better clear out too, Stephen, my lad, while the going's good.'

'I don't know,' said Stephen, 'I think I'll stay.' He was enjoying himself. He was fond of the Cochranes and he liked talking to Bill Farleigh. He had brought home a bottle of sherry, and the dinner was good, the silver shone, everything was as it used to be.

'Well, I've thought it out carefully,' said Colonel Cochrane, 'and what I feel is, why should Mary go on killing herself, slaving away here? Why not have a little comfort for our money at our age? You'll have to bring him over, Laura,' he said, 'and I'll give him a bit of duck shooting.' But his eyes already had the exile's wistfulness. He would be desperately lonely, sitting in the middle of the brown bog reading the London *Times* and the *Field*, and thinking of Wealding. 'Let me,' he said, jumping up to remove the plates. 'Honor and I, if the worst comes to the worst, can always get top wages as a married couple,' said Bill Farleigh, expertly stacking plates at the sideboard. 'I've timed myself washing up, and I don't mind backing myself against a team of your Irish girls out of the bog, Colonel.' Let us help wash up, Laura, said everybody when dinner was over. 'No, please,' said Laura, 'do go into the drawing-room and I'll bring the coffee. Please!' Please let us go on pretending, she meant, seeing Stephen glow and expand and draw up his chair with Bill and the old man in the candlelight. What a damned bore, he had said when Honor telephoned that she was going to change, and he had groaned over hunting up a stiff shirt and finding three moth holes in his evening trousers, but now he was enjoying it. He leant back and crossed his legs luxuriously. Laura made the coffee, surreptitiously tidying up some of the mess, and feeling slightly foolish as she tripped over her long skirts and assisted a flowing chiffon sleeve out of the sink. The silver coffee-tray waited, glittering from the sardonic ministrations of Mrs. Prout, who had attacked it with a banging vigour which plainly masked the thought, Lord, how the gentry do hang on to their ways, poor souls. If it was me, it would be high tea for the lot and done with it. But she had set the table, sniffed the flowers, run up and had a squint at Laura's red dress on the bed, with the somewhat scornful enjoyment of the tourist just about to witness an interesting tribal survival of the aboriginals. Queer, Mrs. Prout's irrepressible eyelid had signalled as she bent her great red face over the sweet peas lifting their antennae in the Leeds china basket, queer but a nice change in its way. And Victoria seemed to share Mrs. Prout's excitement on such occasions, haunting the kitchen where Laura was feverishly banging oven doors, one eye on the clock, prancing round the fascinating table, clamouring, 'Can I stay up? Can I see them? Will Captain Farleigh wear his medals? What are those little bowls for? To wash your *fingers* in? O-oh, how funny!' Thus, thought Laura, carrying the coffee-tray across the hall with great care, mindful of her skirt, and hearing the old hum of voices and laughter from the drawing-room – thus might a child of the tribe, too young to remember the days of the good old ritual feasts, have asked the meaning of the stained bowl and the long knife. Victoria had savoured the occasion voluptuously, crying, 'Oh, how pretty you look!' like a daughter in a story book, when Laura came to say good night, clinging, stroking the old red chiffon respectfully. And no doubt Mrs. Prout had savoured it with equal relish, sitting with Prout in the Tudor rabbit hole down in the village, picturing her in the red dress, him in his shirt front, them old Cochranes and them young Farleighs chinwagging away in the dining-room and polishing off the cheese straws with never a thought, and a blessed old mess mounting up in the kitchen for him and her to clear up afterwards . . .

Now the drawing-room was empty, swept, and garnished, waiting for the next bout. A bee buzzed angrily against the french window, the little clock ticked loudly on the mantel-piece next to the miniature of Victoria, a pink and white, fair-haired English baby waiting on a blue cushion to inherit the earth. It was time to start out and collect the wretched Stuffy. With a sense of luxury, Laura remembered that Victoria was out to tea with the Watsons, so there was no need to hurry back, positively no need to do another thing until this evening. She locked up the house again, thought, Damn! The hens and ducks, and went to mix the food in the shed where, beside the chicken-meal bins, there were a variety of more or less junked objects out of their married life together – Stephen's skis; Victoria's old pram which had been lent to various babies and was now resting; a naked-looking bed pan which had not been required since Laura's lying-in and had somehow anchored on a shelf here next to some old rusty mousetraps; an archery set which Stephen had once bought in a fit of absent-minded enthusiasm at a sale; the stirrup pump and the long-handled shovel for scooping up incendiaries; a tent which, years ago, they had taken with them on a camping holiday in the Dolomites; an ancient Eastern chest marked 'A. Marshall' in painted letters on its lid; and other mementoes now languishing among dust and the smell of chicken food.

XI

The hens lay languidly in the dusty hollows they had scratched under the elders in the paddock. They gathered themselves up in an awkward floundering movement when they saw Laura coming, and ran to meet her, throwing their heads forward in a pushing gesture like skaters taking off on a rink. Sordid, revolting creatures! Why should they be so unattractive, such obvious slave labour whose deaths did not cause one a single pang, when ducks were so charming? She picked up the duck basket and climbed the low wire netting. Here they came waddling, shy, comic, stopping and turning on the single beady impulse, suddenly transfixed quite motionless against the buttercups as though wondering: Is this woman preparing a trap for us? But, reassured, the absurd frieze unfolded itself towards the feeding-trough. There was no drake, there was no cock guarding the hens under the creamy, peppery plates of elder flowers. It was a completely female household to which Stephen returned in the evenings. Even the cat, thought Laura, even Stuffy, shivering and rolling an eye in an abandonment of boneless female hysteria. No wonder that Stephen expanded and glowed, talking to Bill Farleigh in the candlelight. Now you're married we wish you joy, Mrs. Prout had sung the other morning as she shoved the whining carpet sweeper back and forth over the floor, First a girl and then a boy. Ten years after a son and daughter, she had sung, puffing as she bent to gather up a rug and carry it out into the garden. And then the triumphant climax as she began to beat the rug ferociously on the poor daisies – and now, Miss Sally, come out of the water! But such neat mathematics, thought Laura, were sometimes hard to achieve. The years slipped by, wars happened, the hens stalked alone under the elders, the ducks rolled in file, like Lely beauties riding lonely on the waves of their snowy proud bosoms, Stephen frowned over his book in the evenings, she was getting grey, dull, fixed in this trivial routine of cooking the dead slab and cleaning the dirty bath. George Porter's calm blue eyes had delivered the final, the damning sentence. A sofa!

And suddenly, picturing herself standing so tragically clasping the empty bucket in the middle of the duck run, she burst into a fit of laughter. What a fool I am, she thought. Philip would never have made anything out of me, she thought, still smiling as she collected the duck eggs and carried them, rolling slightly at the bottom of the bucket among moist crumbs of mash, back to the shed. Her bicycle also waited there, propped up in a rack with Victoria's. She felt the tyres experimentally before wheeling the machine out into the sunshine, mounting, and riding over the weedy gravel, through the open front gate, and into the deep lane. Absurdly debonair words, she often felt, to describe the humiliating scramble and dab with the foot, the familiar rusty protest of the chain as the pedals went up and down. She had bought the thing for a pound at the beginning of the war, when the Marshalls's house suddenly developed all the less alluring qualities of a desert island. Ah, there's good stuff in it yet, Mr. Jukes at the Crossways Garage had said the other day when he mended a puncture. You don't find this quality in the nasty junk they're turning out to-day, he had said, turning the bicycle upside-down so that the broken green and white strings of the dress guard dangled and it looked almost humanly frail, vulnerable, an elderly female party most unsuitably standing on her head. Stephen had stared and then laughed uncontrollably when he first came home on leave and saw Laura sailing with dignity down the drive. Put it on the scrap heap and buy a new one, he had said not long ago, Jukes has got several decent-looking bikes down in his shop now. But somehow Laura had not done so yet. The old bicycle groaned and grumbled, it resented going uphill, the brakes failed to hold its sudden abrupt forward plunges. But when she looked at it, she thought of it standing waiting for her, propped up in the autumn rain against the village shop or the canteen or the Food Office, and of the bundles it had lugged for her, and of the pallid flicker of light which it used feebly but faithfully to throw before her as she wobbled along the lanes in the blackout. Then she would delay putting it on the scrap heap for a little longer. She rang its bell, a harsh peculiar whirr, as she shot past a couple of women wheeling push-chairs and turned out of the lane into the village.

The familiar scene stated plainly: It is now afternoon. The morning activity had departed with the women carrying their shopping-baskets, and now the square of green grass, roped for cricket in the centre, drowsed in idleness and the cawing of rooks among the Vicarage elms. In one of the cottage gardens someone was cutting a hedge, and the sharp noise of the shears sounded pleasantly positive on the lazy warm air. A group of people in black clothes stood outside the lych-gate of the church. Of course, thought Laura, old Mrs. Pallett's funeral. She recognized none of them except old Mr. Pallett. They were

88

strangers, the men in their best suits, the women in black dresses which looked densely, dustily black against the summer green. They stood chatting with unnatural cheerfulness, with the distrait expressions of travellers who had been shunted by death on to an unfamiliar platform in the middle of their ordinary journey. They gazed at Laura, a woman in a cotton dress riding round the corner on a bicycle, with peculiar intentness, as though they felt, Here is life, here we are back on the reassuring old tracks again. As she bicycled past the Prouts' cottage, sure enough there was a flurry of movement behind the sweet geraniums. Mrs. Prout was peeping from her watch-tower as usual. Now you're married we wish you joy – it made no odds whether she counted anchors made of lilies and wired fern or bridesmaids in sweet-pea colourings. Avid of life, a Shakespearian old nurse bedding the pretty lovers or strewing rosemary over the bier, Mrs. Prout would be spying and wheezing behind her flower pots. And the sight of Laura passing would, Laura knew, distract Mrs. Prout with no feelings of incongruity from the spectacle of sorrowing Pallett sons and daughters to chuckling thoughts of Mrs. Marshall's errand to Barrow Down, of the frailty of straying Stuffy, of the new lot of squirming little varmints who would have to be found homes for somehow round the village. Life and death, for Mrs. Prout, were mingled in one vast, satisfying draught which she gulped in a mouthful and found good. That Stuffy! she would cry, her enormous bosom heaving with merriment, as she twitched back the little curtain to get the last glimpse of Mrs. Pallett's immortality uneasily straggling across the green.

In the window of 'the shop' stood a row of glass jars. Laura braked waveringly, then with decision, and jumped off her bicycle, glancing guiltily over her shoulder. Confronted by that solid clot of sable Palletts, was it an act of disrespect to be thinking of buying some sweets? But they were not looking her way. They were awkwardly moving off, the men beginning to put on their hats, the women to lift their heads and look forward a little more briskly as though the idea of a nice cup of tea had suddenly, revivingly presented itself. In their midst walked the old man, the father, a meek figure like a prisoner among all the big black warders. Laura, propping her bicycle against the chestnut tree, had a sudden perfectly clear picture of Stephen, a thin old man, walking away like that with a womanly Victoria, while she herself lay among the junipers. From being a measureless room with endless arches stretching away, away, life suddenly contracted to a span the size of a hearthrug. But meanwhile, there was a new jar of peppermint humbugs on which Stephen and Victoria doted. Laura opened the door. A bell dangled and jangled from a wire. The tiny dark shop smelled like the inside of a cupboard at home in St. Pol which, for some reason, she could always close her eyes and smell at will. Varnished pine, biscuit crumbs, something vaguely sweet, something sharp as snuff, with an undertone of mice – was it that?

'Good afternoon, Mrs. Marshall,' said young Mrs. Jim.

The daughter-in-law, strange Annabel, the beauty. Good Lord, Stephen had said when he came back from the village, his first look round after he got demobilized, young Jim Trumper picked himself a beauty. Poor chap, he had added, for Jim had gone down on the *Prince of Wales*. The Trumpers had refused to believe, they had gone on hoping. Mrs. Trumper had seen Jim alive in the cards again and again, but it was no good. The oily waters had closed over his red head all right.

Among the packets of Quaker Oats, the cards of corn cures and pen nibs and cachous for the breath, the rakes and the tins of salmon and the rubbishy cotton dresses swinging gently from their hangers in the draught, stood his widow. Sorrow had not caught up with her decorously, as it had with old Mr. Pallett, softening the blow with the broad black shoulders of middle-aged sons and red-faced daughters. Widowhood had not descended on her visibly as it had on Mrs. Bartlett at the Crossroads, whose husband had been such an unconscionable time a-dying that people fled from her broad figure in the village, cravenly shirking the spuriously cheery inquiry, flying from the cold breath of mortality. Jim simply had not returned, that was all. He was there, he was not there. He might never have been, since he had left no child. Mrs. Jim's wifehood had sunk quietly, without a cry, beneath the oily waters.

And how on earth, thought Laura ('Yes, quarter of a pound, please,' she said, feeling for the ration books in her bag), how on earth had Jim, cheerful, ordinary young fellow, managed to pick himself a beauty? This beauty, among all others. How had he concealed the instinct for rightness which had steered him between all the little tuppence-coloured girls, all the little cheap imitations of somebody's hair and bosom and lips on the movies, towards this nose and brow architectural in their love-liness as a church, these unfashionable pale folded lips? It would never be known. The oily waters had closed over the secret. Serene, Mrs. Jim stretched her round white arm for the sweet jar, pronounced 'They're nice,' weighed and deliberated like a Pallas Athene masquerading among the cards of pen nibs and pink cachous.

'It's hot to-day,' she said to Laura. Very hot, they settled. Not so many wasps yet. Ah, but wait for the plum time — mechanically they exchanged a few small coins of country talk while Laura pushed Victoria's ration book towards Mrs. Jim's firm hand.

'Is that nut chocolate?' she said. 'Well, give me a couple of bars too. Take it off Mr. Marshall's book, will you? He does love chocolate.'

'They all do, the men,' said Mrs. Jim. She moved her lips faintly. She picked up the scissors off the counter. 'Did you know I was getting married again?' she asked, snipping carefully.

'No!' said Laura. 'I am so glad. Who is it?' And suddenly she knew the answer. Of course, she thought. George Porter and Mrs. Jim. They were, as the saying goes, meant for each other. There's prospects, George had said, staring ahead over his native heath, thinking of Annabel. She waited, smiling.

'Stanley Rudge,' said Mrs. Jim, snipping carefully. 'You know Mr. Rudge, don't you?' And she dropped the coupons neatly in the box.

'Oh!' said Laura blankly. She could never hide her feelings. You're terrible, Laura, Stephen would say. No thin protective membrane stretched across her emotions, which anyone could read at will, as though they were behind glass. Luckily Mrs. Jim was looking down, exhibiting no interest.

'Of course I know Mr. Rudge,' said Laura blankly.

She picked up the ration books, she stowed them away in her bag. She felt quite shockingly surprised. Before her eyes floated, in a series of distressing visions, a waxed moustache, a bowler hat, a pencil held in stubby fingers, a watchchain festooned over a stomach. Now about the little matter of the ballcock in the downstairs water closet, madam, I'll 'ave my plumber pop round and see to it Monday. Dab went the pencil stump to the waxed moustache, dab went a thick tongue to the pencil stump, dab went the pencil stump to Mr. Rudge's notebook. Now about the little matter of us two getting fixed up, Mr. Rudge would say, and dab! would go the waxed moustache against Mrs. Jim's cheek. Oh horrid impossibility! But she knew that it was perfectly possible. George was the impossibility, the too neat tie-up of two beautiful beings such as one paid one and ninepence to see among cigarette smoke and wet mackintoshes and the witless libidinous whistlings of the Bridbury youths at the Palace. Thus should men be, George had stated calmly, coming out of the cottage in the splendour of high morning, the god carrying the fruit of love in his arms. Thus should life be, stated Mrs. Vyner out of the shadows at her piano, this tender reasoning, this perfect logic, sliding one into the other without a join – so! But thus life is, finally and flatly pronounced Mr. Rudge in the hard, shadowless maturity of full afternoon. He licked the end of pencil, he pressed carefully down on the page in letters so thick that they shone like coal dust, recording the details of length, breadth, height. Out came his foot-rule from the trouser pocket. Flick, dab, dab, and he had it. It was captured in the black notebook for ever.

'When is it to be?' Laura asked. She simply could not utter congratulations, she would not.

'Next month. It can't be too soon for me, I say to Stanley. Such a squash we are here' – Mrs. Jim jerked her head towards the little curtained door behind her – 'now that Cyril's home with his wife and baby, and Effie out of the A.T.S. She and her young man are waiting to get one of the new houses. Wait, wait, nothing but wait nowadays, isn't it?'

She looked at Laura. Laura looked at her. A clock ticked, a bluebottle buzzed, an enormous ginger cat walked majestically into the shop and suddenly, as though his life depended on it, sat down and attacked a patch of fur behind one ear. It is all very well for you, said Mrs. Jim's eyes coldly. You are one of the safe ones, you have a roof and a child. Your man came back. One must take what one can. One is forced to make do, to pick up the crumbs, to be sensible. And all that, the other part, is gone for ever, sunk and drowned beneath the oily waters. She brushed a speck of something off the counter.

'Anyway Stanley has a house,' she said. 'One point in marrying a builder, isn't it? You should have a house.'

'He must be doing well,' said Laura.

'Oh, he is. He's rushed off his feet.'

Yes, Mrs. Prout had said not long ago, shouting above the splash of tap water, that Rudge was doing well. Not making his money over building new houses, Rudge wasn't – *oh*, no, said Mrs. Prout. But doing nicely all the same, in on this, in on that, closing the eye in the right place, opening it in the right place. Sharp, she'd say that for him. Mrs. Bellamy at Hunter's Lodge had a new pink bathroom, though Effie Trumper and her young man were still eating their hearts out for a place to put their good brass double bed which Mrs. Trumper had given them. Ah, Mrs. Prout had cried, wasn't Mrs. Bellamy smart as paint too? All through the war, the food in that house you wouldn't believe, the petrol for the car when nobody else didn't have a drop, and the gin and stuff in the cupboard – oh, didn't Mrs. Sparks at the Leg of Mutton open her eyes when Mrs. Prout told her, and her having to hang out the card 'Not a drop left' on the saloon-bar door night after night! Look at my new pink bathroom, Mrs. Prout, had cried Mrs. Bellamy, running upstairs with her silk stockings twinkling, and goodness only knows how she managed to dress like that with the kewpongs, dressmaker's boxes always arriving, tissue paper on the floor, no questions asked and none answered. Some people have done well out of this war and no mistake, Mrs. Prout had shouted, drawing her red hands out of the water and flopping them, like a couple of wet fishes, into the folds of the roller towel. The sharp ones, the Rudges, the Bellamys, who know how to take good care of Number One. Not the poor softies

94

like you, her kind and scornful eye had said as it surveyed Mrs. Marshall.

'Will that be all for you?' Mrs. Jim asked Laura.

'Yes, that's all to-day.' She paid, she took up the little paper bag and the bars of chocolate. Mrs. Jim stood watching her from behind the counter. She stood with her arms folded in an attitude of statuesque calm. Life is terrifying and uncertain, I have chosen certainty, the intense stillness of her pose seemed to say. Possibly she was perfectly happy. Laura felt suddenly muddled, felt the colour coming into her face, felt a quick impulse to say after all, 'I do hope – I do wish you every sort of happiness.' Cruel and ridiculous words! Mr. Rudge's foot-rule, flicking this way and that, would quickly prove them shallow, flimsy, gimcrack.

'Thanks, Mrs. Marshall,' said Mrs. Jim coolly.

The bell sprang and jangled on its wire as she went out.

XII

She felt uncomfortably hot bicycling out of the village. Now the cottages straggled out into hedges, now came the toll gate, a squatting dwarf with surprised eyes looking down the road, and then the meadows started to spread away towards the high ridge of Barrow Down. The cows moved slowly in the shade of the tall hawthorns, avoiding the line of rusty looped barbed wire as they plunged down to the stream. Behind that barbed wire Doctor Comstock and Colonel Cochrane and Prout had been going to take pot shots at the Germans when they arrived. The strong-point still clung to the top of the bank, looking like a dismal little latrine someone had set down for fun among the foxgloves. Once the jolly monks had ambled across these meadows to fish up their Friday dinner. Now only a heron, grave as an abbot, attended to his fishing among the broad leaves. The pale fluff of meadowsweet and the tarnished buttercups shimmered in the heat and the dancing, humming flies. Was there thunder about? Laura still felt her face burning as it had burnt in the Trumpers' shop. How little one understood anything or anybody, after all. One or two people in one's life really well, and the rest walled up in their separate cells, walking round walled up in darkness which

96

a sentence would suddenly, appallingly, illuminate. If you have any mustard, it would be a good idea to soak your feet – poor Philip! Crash had gone the cell door. Anyway Stanley has a house, Mrs. Jim had said, staring at her, hating her, declaring on the side of certainty. Will that be all? Yes, that's all. And there they were, walled up in their separate selves again, Laura Marshall and Annabel Trumper, unable to stir hand or foot or find a chink through which their lips could send warnings or pity or reassurance. Old Rudge! Stephen would say to-night when she told him. Well, I'm damned! Old Rudge! She felt frightfully depressed.

Now came a slight hill curving up from the meadows, shaded by the great arms of the oaks. She got off and began to push the bicycle uphill. The little bag of sweets joggled in the bicycle basket, and she thought, Should she have one? This dreadful sweet tooth, this base and constant craving, while before the war she had passed *marrons glacés* melting in their fluted cups, sugared almonds, parterres of crystallized red and white fruit on angelica twigs, without giving them a second thought. But now, this awful craving. Stephen was the same. At home, her father hid his sweet ration in a tin in the brown snuggery, retired and ate with private greed behind *The Times* after lunch. It was no good. She stopped, opened the bag, and took a humbug. Behind her, clear across the meadows, the Wealding clock struck the hour.

Now, she thought, Victoria will be closeted with Miss Trasker, ponderously pursuing 'Water Lily Elves' from toadstool to toadstool. How they limped, those elves, how they pounded on fairy clogs away from Victoria's inky fingers. *One*-two-three, *one*-two-three, Miss Trasker would murmur, bending her short-sighted face, dedicated, raptly earnest, closer to Victoria's solid shoulder, Attention to the slurs, dear. Was it possible that

Mrs. Vyner's music had ever started from such beginnings? And was she, Laura, ridiculous to have Victoria given all the little graces of the Herriot world, the light foot, the agile finger, the easy manner, when it seemed perfectly clear that she would have to work seriously for her living if she happened to escape being blown into little pieces? This was the ugly drawing-room in which Victoria would be called upon to perform 'Water Lily Elves.' But it was no use worrying, no use reading the papers and worrying. Stephen read the papers and sat frowning, thinking, in the evenings as she sat opposite him, sewing away at the basket of mending which perpetually gushed out its bowels beside her chair, and outside the window the bats and the moths flitted over the tobacco flowers and the stocks. What was the use? She was luckily always too tired to read much, the serious words jumbled and made soothing jabberwocky nonsense. When I think how you were brought up, Mrs. Herriot had said reproachfully, conjuring up geranium-urned terraces over Italian lakes and tennis-party lemonade by the sweep of her knitting-needle. So might Laura address Victoria at some unimaginable juncture of the frightening future, citing the bronze dancing-sandal, the French lesson, the one-two-three with Miss Trasker, which had prepared her for a world full of horrors. For a second, plodding up the hill, feeling the comforting warmth of the humbug in her cheek, Laura experienced the familiar sinking sensation in the pit of her stomach, a black emptiness. Well, it was no use worrying. She had reached the top of the slope. She went through the scramble and dab motions again, sailed on.

In these fields they were haymaking. Half a dozen German prisoners were working with the farmer, Mr. Pratt, and a couple of his men. The Germans were mostly young fellows, and they had stripped to the waist. They were very sunburnt. One blond boy's chest, against which a small silver disc dangled, and his muscular arms looked a Red Indian colour. How did they manage it in this disastrous summer which was only now appearing to relent, to throw them some hot sun and blue skies? Those who were working near the fence caught sight of Laura and stared at her with the desperate interest of the marooned male in a skirt, in any skirt. An older man, about Stephen's age, wore glasses and had a peering, bookish-looking face which made his occupation seem strange. I wish they would all go home, thought Laura. They always made her uncomfortable and wretched as though it were somehow her fault. She tried to get past as quickly as possible on the squeaking old bicycle, but she could feel that they were staring at her still, watching her out of sight with that deadly silent concentration. They were so horribly silent. When the Canadians were up at the big house, they had always whistled or shouted a cheerful Hiya! as Laura went by, an automatic signal which simply stated without any particular hope, I am a man, you are a woman. They had even yelled Hiya, toots! at Mrs. Prout, who had shaken with Rabelaisian merriment and bridled as she heaved past on her bicycle. But the Germans were silent in their degraded patched clothing, like denizens of another world who had lost the right or the power to communicate. A high hedge of dusty dog-roses and bramble flowers hid them. Thank goodness! She could relax.

A wall began to run alongside the road, tall and stoutly built of stone and flint. Keep out! it seemed to say, but in a couple of places army trucks had taken no notice, had bashed gaps in it, and landed drunk and askew on the soft slippery pine needles. The trucks had gone, but the gaping holes remained. The wall was also beginning to give up slightly on its own account, sagging slightly here, shedding stone and flint there. But this stretch of the road was deliciously cool in the damp-smelling shade of the pines and the beeches. Two relations of the wood-pigeon Laura had heard that morning were purring away in Mrs. Cranmer's woods, I love you, Lulu, over and over, the lazy sound of summer. Ahead was the lodge, with that bush of tiny toy roses in its little garden which Victoria always looked for when they passed in the car. Before Laura reached it, a man stepped out of the copse on the other side of the road, a dog at his heels, and stood waiting for her.

'Hallo, Laura,' he said.

'Edward! I didn't know you were down,' she said.

She got off the bicycle and stood smiling. She felt awfully glad to see him. Edward Cranmer's spaniel crossed the road heavily to inspect her shoes, wag his tail, and lift a soft, gummy eye, dripping with the rheum of age and goodwill to all men. He moved as though his feet hurt him, exactly like a gouty old man.

'We're here for a week or two,' Edward said, 'trying to straighten things out a bit. Helen is down too.'

'It's all settled?'

'Haven't you seen the papers to-day? The photograph is in them.'

No, said Laura, she had not had time to see the papers yet. But of course she had known for a long time, ever since the morning when Mrs. Prout had arrived panting, bursting with the burden of her song, the amazing theme of which was contained in the line: The Cranmers were giving up. With no more excitement could Mrs. Prout have stated that Barrow Down had stalked off in the night, taken its famous tuft of wind-bitten trees, and removed itself to the other side of the county. Oh, she would never have believed it, Mrs. Prout had cried, and needed endless cups of tea to soften her disbelief. Wealding without the Cranmers – was it possible? Instead of the family up at the Manor, something which called itself the National Trussed – so Prout had had it from Fowler, the carter, who had had it from Dummer at one of the old lady's farms. The village hummed with it. At the Leg of Mutton they talked of nothing else. Was it a good job, was it a bad job? Some said one, some said the other. But one and all had a curious sensation, as though a stout wall had gone and a draught was catching them in the neck. Wealding would be different, on that there was no argument.

He was just, Edward said, going up to the house for tea. Why didn't Laura come too?

'They'd love to see you,' he said. 'I was asking my mother last night how you all were.'

'Well –' She hesitated. But why not? Stuffy could wait. So they started walking together, Edward Cranmer wheeling Laura's old bicycle for her and looking rather absurd doing so, for he was immensely tall and thin and had elegant long hands which looked as though they should be laid against furred velvet or the red robes of a court dignitary. For a second, glancing sideways at him, a likeness to somebody else, seen recently, teased Laura, until she thought, Of course! The German prisoner working in the hayfield had had the same sort of fine-drawn, short-sighted face, born to browse, in the green light of tree-shaded eighteenth-century rooms, on the fusty herbiage of old books. The hands were Edward's only link-up with the family, Laura had thought the last time she was at Cranmer and had been round the pictures. For the same strong family face repeated itself again and again along the faded red damask walls, blue-eyed, straight-nosed, blooming with the physical beauty that comes from generations of little thinking and much strenuous outdoor exercise. Their long fingers, laid lightly on a satin bosom or the hilt of a sword, had been given a flattering indoor fragility which their fine high colours, whipped into their full cheeks by stinging air on a hunting morning, had only too plainly denied.

Ah! Mrs. Herriot had said, her head on one side before a portrait. She had been there on that occasion, asked up to lunch with Laura and Stephen. And it really had been an occasion, the war was over, the Canadians had gone, the lunch seemed perfect as ever though there was only Fowler, Mrs. Cranmer's old maid, to creak round with the dishes which Mrs. Bunt from the lodge had helped to serve up in the great echoing stone-flagged kitchen. Some other people were there – a red-faced old man in tweeds, a famous soldier and explorer, and his wife. They owned one of the most beautiful Jacobean houses in the county, but it was shut up now, and they lived in one of the estate cottages. Mrs. Herriot had enjoyed herself at lunch, talking to the charming old man, and she enjoyed herself later, going round the pictures with Laura. Ah! she said, her head on one side, as though she felt perfectly at home among all these comely, blooming men and women who had looked so confidently into the eyes of the painter. They were really splendid; their red-and-blue laced coats proclaimed that they had done their duty well by England, and a childlike look in their slightly prominent eyes testified to the healthy simplicity of their pleasures – a good bit of horseflesh beneath them, the damp leaf-mould smell of their woods, the banked fire and the sleeping dogs at the end of the long day. Ah! said Mrs. Herriot, feeling herself among friends, but then her glance had gone rapidly to Edward Cranmer, talking with Lady Bruce across the room. What a change was here, her glance had said to Laura, who chanced to catch it. For Edward had no bloom, his face was marked with the harsh discipline of thought, which also seemed to have marked his body so that he carried himself with an ugly, scholarly stoop. What a dry stick to spring from the base of this splendid old tree! So Mrs. Herriot had plainly, disapprovingly reflected before she moved on to the next picture, a handsome young woman who had been painted in her riding-habit, her spaniel's long tresses mingling with her own.

He was not like his father, the old squire, Mrs. Prout had often said to Laura. Though he was pleasant enough, he was not a patch on old Mr. Cranmer, whose hawks and hounds, waist-coats, sharp tempers, kind dealings, and lusty hitting on the green in Wealding cricket week had become a village legend. It would die soon, for only the old people remembered and some-times spoke of him. Radical or no, Mrs. Prout had said, you had to respect him. Everyone had been sorry when he went, and was drawn to church by his own Percherons on a farm wagon, just as though he were a truss of the dried grass which the Vicar (old Mr. Judge, who had been there before Mr. Vyner) read about with his surplice blowing in the wind by the graveside. And now Mr. Edward lived in Cambridge and wrote learned books, some said, and watched birds, Wealding children had reported, meeting him on spring evenings mooning along by the willows and the shivering reeds, his field-glasses slung round his neck. Catch the old squire watching birds, except down the shiny barrel of a gun! (There had been a rare popping from the Cranmer woods, and a rare coming and going of motors and ladies' maids and dogs every autumn in the old days, Mrs. Prout had recollected as she crawled her way, exposing a glimpse of knotted blue flesh above the sagging stocking, over Laura's bathroom floor.) But to everyone's surprise, Mr. Edward had done well in the war, chucking up his professors and such, get-ting himself a couple of medals and a permanently stiff leg in North Africa.

He limped more than usual, pushing Laura's bicycle up the drive, past the lodge where Mrs. Bunt's canaries were making their cages quake up and down and the air shudder with their top notes. It had been hot work walking round the farms, he said, over to Dummer's, through the chestnut plantations to Pratt's and the rest. What did they think about it all? asked Laura.

'I think, on the whole, they're sorry,' he said. 'They like my mother, you know.'

'But she'll still be here?'

'Oh yes, she'll still be here. She and Aunt Sophia will go on living in the flat they're making in the stables wing – they move in next week, probably.'

The house, he said, would be used partly as a holiday hostel, partly as an agricultural training centre for boys.

'I'm glad it's not going to be quite dead,' he said. 'It's a good place to be young in.'

He turned his head this way and that, looking quietly at a fat pony standing swishing its tail in one of the paddocks, at the woods and the distant river, at the great bulk of the house beginning to come into sight between the dark level slats of the cedars.

'It's the only possible thing for all these places,' he said. 'I could never afford to live here even if I wanted to. You can't imagine what a relief it is, Laura, to get it all settled.'

'All the same, I can't imagine Cranmer without you,' Laura said.

'Perhaps we've been here long enough,' he said. 'It's time for a change. And look at it as it is, rotting away! That was what really broke one's heart.'

He leant her bicycle against the wall near the myrtle bush, grown from the cutting of some Cranmer bride's bouquet, he had told her once. Everything had its tradition, its story. The past, which in the Herriots' house was pressed like a dry butterfly between the glass of Edwardian photograph frames, could be seen here as something living which did not stop abruptly, but went on, stretching out to the present, on into the future. Even the Canadian huts, grouped in the park beyond the haha, had somehow been assimilated, become the contribution of another war, just as previous ones had added the rusty cannon balls along the terrace and the little obelisque of victory which a patriotic Cranmer had erected at the end of the wedge cut through the woods down to the river.

The house, thought Laura, looked completely uninhabited, rotting away, basking and staring with blank eyes at the weedy gravel and the lawns, which were now hayfields. It had, for a moment, a disconcerting air of being already a ruin, quite hollow behind the plum-pink bricks and the Cranmer hatchments. Rooks cawed, flopping in their crazy-looking settlement in the big old trees; neither she nor Edward spoke for a moment, and Laura had a feeling that the silence would surely be broken up by the boots of the custodian, popping out of his little room, wiping tea from the ends of his moustache, and starting to gabble about the dining-hall and the site of the old keep. When Edward spoke, she jumped nervously.

XIII

There were packing-cases in the hall. Doors stood ajar on shuttered twilight, on vague shapes hanging in holland bags from the ceiling, on larger shapes muffled beneath dust-sheets like groups of statuary waiting to be unveiled by a lady with a bouquet. After the warmth and the buzz outside, the place struck chilly as a church. The dog's claws tapped confidently on the oak floors ahead of them.

'That's where your mother had her working parties,' Laura said, nodding towards a door.

'Did you come to those?' he asked absently.

'As much as I could.'

Fluff off the white winceyette, she remembered, had prickled the nose and made her sneeze. Mrs. Vyner had ripped away at one machine, Honor Farleigh at the other. They sighed, they stitched, they lifted needles towards the light filtering greenly through the high mullions. The news was bad, the news was good, Mr. Churchill had said, and the food – ah, the food! How are you getting on, Mrs. Prout? Mrs. Cranmer would cry from the head of the long table where she presided, her stick against her chair, the old spaniel stinking and scratching his eczema at her feet. Nicely, madam, thank you, Mrs. Prout would reply.

Radical or no, she squeezed a 'madam' for Mrs. Cranmer when she turned up and sat, panting from the exertion of pedalling up the long avenue, slyly storing away nuggets of gossip in her vast bosom, shaking out the striped pyjama trousers and eyeing the dangling legs with an awful stare which seemed to fill them. Lord, she would say later to Laura, how that old dog does smell, he ought to be put away. And the house – what a sight when you thought of it in the old days, the footman and all, and now only that old Fowler doddering round with Mrs. Bunt from the lodge. It was a nasty pull up the avenue for her heart, Mrs. Prout would say. She wouldn't go again. But she turned up next week all right. She enjoyed it. There was something soothing about it, Laura always felt, as though they were repeating some classic pattern which went on recurring for ever in different fancy dresses, the group of women sitting sewing round the lady of the house while their men were at the wars, fighting the Trojans or the Turks or the Nazis. Men must fight and women must sew – of course in this war women had fought too. They had flown aeroplanes, they had been bombed on gun sites, they had struggled in the dreadful equality of icy water among drowning men. Military buttons had marched up Effie Trumper's bosom, Air Force blue had all too insecurely disguised Mavis Porter in doublet and hose. But still the other women had sat stitching and folding, making ready, storing away, in quiet old houses like Mrs. Cranmer's. There was something soothing about it, the ritual gesture which said, While you destroy, we build up, we stitch and fold quietly in the inner courtyard which is the true centre of the house. It had been easy, in an idle moment, to picture Mrs. Cranmer's massive chins bound round with linen bands, the long table and the striped winceyette legs and Mrs. Vyner, bending her damp-looking pale face over the Singer, all giving place to the loom and the slowly growing greens and blues and greys of the tapestry forest.

A dark old Italian mirror gleamed from a gilt frame twisted like roots under water. Laura glanced towards it, suddenly thinking uneasily of her hair, her hands. She must look a fright, and one did not, somehow, appear before Mrs. Cranmer looking a fright.

But it was too late to do anything about it. Slightly ahead of her, Edward opened a door and said, 'I've brought a visitor.' The library looked as though the electric lights were on, but it was the afternoon sunlight striking a pale yellow glow from gilt and calf bindings of the books towering up to the high painted ceiling. In the midst of death done up in little holland shrouds, said the room, we are in life. More dogs uncurled themselves from the rugs and flew to meet Edward. 'My dear Laura,' said Mrs. Cranmer, 'what a pleasant surprise!' The three ladies were already at tea. In the corner of the big velvet sofa, Miss Sophia Cranmer beaked like a startled old parrot, a bit of sandwich hanging like a large seed from one claw. She smiled dimly. But she does not remember in the least who I am, thought Laura. The room was deliciously cool. In its beauty and dignity it denied everything – the weedy terrace outside the open windows, the packing-cases, the holland bags, old Fowler boiling a kettle somewhere in the empty vast kitchens, the drive torn up by the soldiers' lorries, change barging in through the holes in the solid old wall. Nothing is wrong, said the room. The little group round the tea-table seemed to float in the rich light, huddled together like survivors on a raft.

And nothing is wrong, Mrs. Cranmer seemed to declare also as they talked. Not a word indicated that this was one of the last times that she would sit here, pouring out from the massive tea-service, leaning back and looking at Laura with her amused old eyes. She spoke of everything but that. She was dressed as usual in black. When she went out, she had a way of snatching up an ancient tweed shooting-cape of Mr. Cranmer's and throwing it round her shoulders. Laura had met her one day, flapping across the fields towards one of her farms, stooping, prodding the earth familiarly with her stick, stumping on among a white and brown and piebald sea of dogs. Before she got too lame, she gardened in shocking boots and a hat like a bee skip. She did not care a button how she looked. But at dinner parties before the war, in black velvet and diamonds, she could look like a queen.

'More tea, Sophia?' she called loudly to her sister-in-law.

'She didn't hear,' said Helen, leaning forward and repeating the question, in her cool distinct voice, closer to old Miss Cranmer's nodding auburn front. Then she sat back and went on talking about housing difficulties in Cambridge. Stephen thought her rather charming, Mrs. Herriot had been greatly struck when they met that day at lunch. Such perfect taste, Mrs. Herriot had thought, the neat figure, the single string of pearls, the fine hair waved back in scallop shells from the brow. Your stocking, darling, has a ladder in it, she had said briskly to Laura as she got into the car going home. Impossible to imagine Helen untidy, ruffled, letting things boil over on the stove. She had run something in London all through the war with, everyone said, wonderful competence. But what, Laura could not help wondering, had made Edward lift his short-sighted eyes from the page, see the limp brown hair, the face so correctly pretty that one had to remember it all over again each time one saw it, and think to himself, This is the one? They had been married twelve years and had no chick, no child, only the little Chinese dog snoring on Helen's lap.

Ah, but Mrs. Cranmer had her griefs as well as the rest of us, had cried Mrs. Prout who had herself lost four sons, reared four. It had seemed to afford Mrs. Prout, sighing and wheezing, a mysterious satisfaction, the idea that Mrs. Cranmer had been bowed with the common grief though she never showed it, though her voice rang clear and unfaltering, and the men said she was a caution, you couldn't put anything past her. They were all frightened of her, Mrs. Prout said to Laura – Pratt at Lower Farm, Dummer, Stokes, the whole lot of them. But sorrow hardened some, softened others. The eldest son, Henry, had died suddenly at school, a lovely boy, everybody's favourite. Mr. Robert had been killed out in Africa, where he went big-game shooting with a party of friends. There had been two other sons who died in infancy. And now the fresh-cheeked, full-bodied Cranmer stock had dwindled and thinned into Edward, sitting there by his wife, pulling the little dog's tawny lion locks. 'I had a battle with that old scoundrel Rudge at the Wealding parish meeting over the new houses,' Mrs. Cranmer was saying, and he was laughing, teasing her. 'Nonsense!' she said, laughing too, and the door opened and in came Fowler carrying a tray. From some window she must have seen Edward and Laura, for she had brought fresh tea and sandwiches.

'Hallo, Fowler,' said Laura.

'Good afternoon, madam,' said Fowler.

She was a small, thin woman, Mrs. Cranmer's old maid. Hiya, toots! Hiya, Miss Fowler! the Canadians used to call, grinning, when they saw her toddling down the lime avenue to have tea with her crony Mrs. Bunt at the lodge, among the yelling canaries and innumerable photographs of the Family. She had never taken any notice of their insufferable impudence, uncalled for however far they had come to fight for anybody, she would say to Mrs. Bunt as they sat together drinking a nice cup, watched by Mr. Henry chubbily bestriding his first Shetland, Mr. Robert in his uniform at Sandhurst, Mrs. Cranmer with a muff against an Edwardian snow scene, Mr. Cranmer on old Pericles among his hounds, and the rest. Thank goodness, she had said to Mrs. Bunt as the last singing, rowdy truckload rolled away that day, not knowing that worse was to come. Thank goodness it's over, she had said, going off to look over Mrs. Cranmer's evening dresses and scrutinize her sables for the moth, for would not everything now be as it used to be? Back would come the men into their brass buttons or baize aprons, back would come the girls into their print dresses. And about time, she had said to Mrs. Bunt, for her feet ached terribly, she could hardly lie in bed at night for the pains in her back. Fowler, whose job had been to mend the torn lace on the tea gown and clean the ruby rose with a little brush, now lay in bed and ached all over. Sometimes at night, she had told Mrs. Bunt, feeling herself creaking, listening to the house creaking and going to pieces, worrying about the falling plaster and the swaddled furniture and the damage those dratted Canadians were doing to the place – sometimes Fowler had wondered how much longer she could keep things going for Mrs. Cranmer and Mr. Edward, who after all did not care. And it had been no good, as it turned out.

'Good afternoon, madam,' she said to that Mrs. Marshall, who had come calling without a hat, without any stockings on her long legs. She set down a plate, collected an empty one, glanced over the table. Yes, they had all they wanted. Mrs. Cranmer was laughing with Mr. Edward over something. Laugh away, then, a voice said quite wildly inside Fowler's breast. But she went quietly out with her tray.

'You know we're moving out this week,' Mrs. Cranmer said suddenly to Laura. She lay back, scratching the old spaniel's ribs with the point of her stick. He grunted with pleasure, his rheumy little eye rolled upwards in ecstasy. She and Fowler, Edward, Helen, Mrs. Bunt, Bunt with his hammer and nails, all of them had been working away as hard as they could go, taking Cranmer apart. A dreadful job, she said, when a house had been there so long, when so many people had saved and stored everything carefully for centuries, letters, journals, estate accounts, locks of hair, shreds of silk, sentimental rubbish of all sorts. Some of the furniture was being sold, some would go to Edward, the best of the pictures to the nation, and a few into the new abode with her and Sophia and Fowler. For instance, that – she jerked the stick towards the conversation piece above the fireplace.

'I'm glad,' Laura said, 'I always loved that one.'

'Peregrine was fond of it,' she said.

The two ladies, sisters perhaps, one in sea-green satin, the other in flounces of yellow satin, conversed with the gentleman with the gun while, in the background, a little negro boy played with a tremendous parrot in a cage. Over the three faces, blooming as though they could have downed a leg of mutton apiece without any trouble, and the grinning turbaned face of the little negro, played the rich, soaking light of the long English afternoon which had seemed as though it would last for ever.

And the next thing would be, Mrs. Cranmer said, the boys would move in.

'You won't hear them, round in the stable wing,' Helen said, 'it should be quiet.'

'I don't mind if I do,' Mrs. Cranmer said. 'I like boys. There always used to be dozens of boys round the place, Edward – you and your friends, and Robert's and Henry's.'

'It will be like old times for you,' Helen said, 'with hundreds of Edwards, darling, dozens of Roberts and Henrys.' She smiled, stroking the little Chinese dog's ears.

Such a pity, a sad pity, Mrs. Vyner had said one December afternoon to Laura as they decorated the church for Christmas. Such a pity for Mrs. Cranmer, Mrs. Vyner had mourned through a gag of green twine as she crawled beneath the brass eagle reading-lectern. No grandchild for Mrs. Cranmer to be splashed by Mr. Vyner at the font, no future stretching ahead for the Cranmers whose past was all round them now, in the little church smelling of fresh-cut evergreens, in brass underfoot and marble on the wall and ruffed Elizabethan stone, piously kneeling with a whole string of miniature ruffed immortality queuing up behind them. Those were the days for the fine large families, Mrs. Vyner had said. No accidents big-game shooting or sudden fevers at school could make much of a hole in that solid little platoon of heirs down on their knees behind the paternal and maternal boot soles. But now look what was happening to so many of the good old families, Mrs. Vyner had mumbled sadly through her mouthful of twine. Played out, petering out! While to make it still harder – she sank her voice – people like those awful Porters bred and bred like rabbits in their dreadful cottage. The empty church, beginning to fill with the cold wash of winter twilight, had echoed with metallic noises when Laura or Mrs. Vyner dropped a pair of scissors or set down a water-can, as though men were working in a deep mine shaft below the fifteenth-century Cranmer brasses.

And Mrs. Prout, who from her watch-tower behind the sweet geraniums seemed to spy into every bed in Wealding, had often shaken her head over the same enjoyable theme. Mrs. Edward was staying up at Cranmer again, she would say. She had watched her going into the post office to buy some stamps, but not a sign, not a flicker of hope, a barren fig tree in her neat tweed suit if ever Mrs. Prout saw one. Mark my words,

Mrs. Prout would cry as she and Laura heaved the morning mattress together, you'll never see chick nor child there.

'Come along and I'll show you the flat, Laura,' Mrs. Cranmer said, groping for her stick and heaving herself out of the chair. She took Laura's arm; Edward and Helen strolled after them. At the door Laura glanced back at Miss Cranmer, who had been left sitting in the corner of the velvet sofa. She did not seem to notice their departure. She was staring into space, her hands folded in her lap, her head twitching now and then like a dog who dreams. Her small figure looked lost in the great glowing room, swimming in the light of the summer afternoon. The group over the fireplace gazed down at her with well-fed, amiable arrogance, declaring that they were English ladies and gentlemen who would for ever inherit the earth. Thus should life be, they said, the green garden and the trout rising in the river, the white hand curled against the sea-green silk, the dead wild duck dangling, the jolly little slave crouching beside the cage of the huge flaunting crimson and yellow bird. Thus will life always be, stated their healthy confident faces. But in a minute there was nobody in the room but Aunt Sophia.

XIV

Out in the garden, the other two strolled off in the opposite direction. Edward said something to his wife, she tucked her hand in his arm, and he laughed. No doubt it was in many ways a perfectly successful marriage, thought Laura. Look how frightfully wrong you often are about people, Stephen would say, always liking the wrong ones, imagining them unhappy when they are perfectly happy. Helen, she thought, is probably very clever at arranging for Edward to be left in peace with his books and his writing-table, at collecting the people he likes, at lighting softly shaded lamps and sitting with needlework, keeping restfully silent. For they strolled off very peaceably, somehow looking extremely together, her hand inside his arm. Perhaps Edward had known what he was doing when he said to himself, There! This is the one! The spaniel, after a slight hesitation between Edward and his mother, ambled after them and the little dog, drooping his ringlets to the earth.

'It's really quicker going round the outside way,' Mrs. Cranmer said.

But it was not particularly quick even so, for there was so much of the house to walk round. Laura looked up at its windows, feeling oppressed by the great stretch of mauvish brick looming like the side of a ship against the blue and the sluggish, fat clouds. It seemed to lean and slip towards her, as though it were sailing through space away from its moorings. All those windows, she thought in horror. For the rest of her life, now, she would see things from the point of view of cleaning them. Confronted by a masterpiece of architecture, she would think merely, How much floor to sweep, how many stairs to run up and down. The world had contracted to domestic-house size, always whispering to the sound of somebody's broom. The old house rode so superbly on the green billow of its parkland. Where, in that lovely hulk, lurked Fowler, who alone stood on the burning deck whence all but she had fled? Was that a whisk of ghostly cap and apron at a window? But it was a pigeon fluttering down from a jut of mossy roof where a row of them sat purring and sidling with tiny steps, tucking back their heads behind the soft curved breastplates of their feathers.

'Pleasant noise,' Mrs. Cranmer said. 'I shall hear them in my new room.'

Ladders already stood against the wall. A painter's white coat hung on a hook, melancholy with the queer human sadness of the abandoned possession which says in a fold, or in the limp curved fingers of a dropped glove, You have deserted me. The workmen had gone home to tea. As Mrs. Cranmer had said, the sunlight flooded into these rooms. Her stick pointed this way and that – here the family group with the parrot, here her desk, a big one, for she still dealt with much of the estate business herself. She liked boys, her nurseries had always been strewn with lead soldiers and toy railway tracks. And she had continued to prefer, guessed Laura, the conversation of men. She missed the Canadian officers who had been stationed in the house, she said. Such interesting, fine young men, they had dined with her every Thursday, and drunk her cellar dry – heavens, how Fowler had detested them! She would still enjoy going down to one of the farms and standing talking to Dummer or Stokes in the rain. She would enjoy sitting at the big solid desk, going over accounts with the bailiff. There was something masculine about her, Laura thought, the authority of one who had always been accustomed to make the decisions. She looked around, up and down, observant beneath the heavy lids.

'We shall be pretty snug here,' she said indifferently. The pigeons cooed and cooed, plushy and thick in their throats. A board creaked under her weight as she stumped down the stairs. Rudge had promised, she said, to have the bath in by the end of the week. Everything waited for the bath, it was impossible to move in without that. Yet when she had first married, there was only one bathroom in the whole house, and they had managed very comfortably. People are cleaner to-day, she said, but I don't know that I like them any better.

'That old rascal Rudge,' she said. He knew what he wanted, he would end by buying up all Wealding. She sounded amused. She and Rudge, Laura thought with surprise, would get on very well indeed. Now about that little matter of the bath, Mr. Rudge would say confidentially. He would not be scared of her, as Pratt and the rest of the men were scared, standing turning and turning their caps in their hands, looking hangdog and chapfallen. He would size her up quickly with his small blood-shot eyes, keeping a flat thumb on his foot-rule as though about to measure how far he could go, to chip the surface with a grubby nail and find out if it was only veneer or the solid old stuff which, after all, he would have to admire. Like a cocky little bird, waxed, ruffling, wonderfully insolent, he would stand his ground before her. We all 'ave to wait our turns now, madam. Even Mrs. Cranmer of Cranmer Manor, owing to the admirable sideslip which the world has now taken, must wait her turn like the rest, his bloodshot little eye would say. It would satisfy some deep emotion located beneath the festooned watchchain to remember that his father had been a bricklayer, his mother a servant girl, he had often gone hungry in his youth, but here he was rising, rising, a handsome new villa bought for himself the other day, more land being added bit by bit, and he stood on the faded Aubusson cabbage roses with his legs apart, telling Mrs. Peregrine Cranmer that she must wait her turn with the rest. And yet he would like her, he would respect her. Some urbanity which he did not quite understand, some calm but smiling obtuseness over the situation as he saw it, would leave him feeling vaguely as though she, after all, had done him the favour. They would part with mutual liking and heightened colours, thinking The old rascal, the old battle-axe.

Marrying that good-looking daughter-in-law of the Trumpers, so she had heard, said Mrs. Cranmer. They were out in the flagged yard, passing the empty boxes and the coach-house where a door stood ajar on canary and black paint, spidery shafts tilted upwards. And she would understand that too, felt Laura. She would never undervalue worldly success, not she. She would have no patience with Mrs. Herriot's hyper-fastidious attitude towards money as something to be enjoyed but not mentioned, which fell naturally as the gentle dew from heaven upon the honourable recipients beneath. To Mrs. Cranmer, a bargain was a bargain, and she could be shrewd as an old peasant calculating the value of a cow.

'An excellent thing,' she said reasonably. Money was not to be sneezed at. Indeed no! They had come again to the front of the house. There was no sign of Edward and Helen. Mrs. Cranmer stood for a moment, her hand resting against a mossy urn, looking silently down the broad ride towards the oddly Eastern little pyramid in the park, and beyond it to the great massive trees and the park-like English fields. Everything was so still, the clatter of some farm machine a couple of miles away sounded near.

'I always thought that if the Germans had come, I'd have had a good view from here,' Mrs. Cranmer said.

'What ages ago that seems,' Laura said.

All that summer, in memory, had seemed to be like this one day, burning, blazing. The calm, gentlemanly voice on the wireless had said this and that. Paris fell, the Germans were in Paris, and she stood with a basket picking peas, calmly picking fat green peas. Victoria ran about in a little bathing-suit with an anchor embroidered on its bib, watering her own toes with a small red watering-can. Everything was burning, blazing, but she stood mechanically pulling the fresh, creaking pods off the rows, thinking, I'll hate these things all my life. But she did not. She adored them, and had frequently picked them since without a thought.

'What would have happened?' Mrs. Cranmer mused. 'I often wonder. I suppose it would have been disastrous. But I would have liked —'

What would she have liked, Laura wondered as she did not go on. To do something violently active, instead of sitting at the head of the long table, crying, How are you getting on, Mrs. Prout? It was possible to imagine Mrs. Cranmer in another age, directing the heating of boiling water, heaving rocks over the battlements, even stumping out herself with the troops. Yes, she would have liked that! But she had been tied helplessly to her corner of the big decaying house, over which the

119

German planes grumbled every night, peaceful and regular as a line of buses, scorning it, going on to drop their loads on the cities. She had never had even that taste of danger. And she had sewed so atrociously at her working parties, handling the work with the awkwardness of the woman who had never in her life been asked to sew on a button, and whose tastes ran naturally to walking across turnip fields in the rain, or to getting down on all fours under a tangle of little boys on her nursery floor. But to this clumsiness she had added a sort of fierceness of her own, frowning, jabbing the needle back and forth as though she hated the innocent pyjama coat, hated this sitting here blah-blah-ing with a pack of women while England was fighting for her life. Take this, take that, accursed fate which found me old and a woman, had flashed Mrs. Cranmer's needle. My God, Honor Farleigh used to groan as she packed the parcels to be sent to the depot in Bridbury, this must be one of hers! We can't – we really can't send such a frightful – And Mrs. Vyner would roll it up and pop it in her bag, to take home and unpick and remake Mrs. Cranmer's sampler of fury with the fates.

She stood looking at the view, unpossessively, seeming to appraise like a casual tourist who never expected to come this way again. And already the house, thought Laura, had an impersonal look. It seemed to say, I have no more secrets, I shall have no more stories. Visitors to Wealding, driving along the lower road from which one could see Cranmer standing lovely above the water meadows, would ask their host intelligently, What is that? instead of Who lives there? For so obviously its personal life had ended, it would resound in future with the cheerful echoing noises of collective living, the sound of a great Amen, the clatter of forty feeding as one. Who wrote that? Laura wondered absently. She could not remember. Her mind was a ragbag, in which scraps of forgotten brightness, odd bits of purple and gold, were hopelessly mixed up with laundry lists and recipes for doing something quick and unconvincingly delicious with dried egg. You used, her mother would say reproachfully, to be so well up in things. Soon I must read some good books, she thought, I must keep awake in the evenings long enough to read some poetry again.

But when she turned back to Mrs. Cranmer, a stout old woman without beauty or grace or fashion, for some reason she began to think quite naturally in poetical images; she saw Mrs. Cranmer standing reassuring as a rock or a tower in the frightening uncertainty of everything which could turn her stomach to black water as she bicycled along on a fine summer day. The position in Trieste clung to the wet fish skin, Stephen frowned as they sat together listening to the wireless speaking suavely of alarming things, but Mrs. Cranmer, by simply standing screwing up her eyes at a view, seemed to say, Be not afeared. How did that go? Be not afeared, the isle is full of noises – something of that kind, in her silence and the lift of her head, Mrs. Cranmer contrived to say. The fancy only lasted a second. She moved, she became once more a stout old woman limping slowly back towards the great house which appeared to be drifting away, away, a deserted ship with its portholes blind, its chimneys smokeless, across the deep blue of the sky.

The others had still not reappeared when Laura wheeled her bicycle from behind the bride's myrtle bush. Perhaps they had sat down somewhere, for a moment only, to look at the light on the river and the beech woods, while Edward smoked, while she said nothing much in the soothing way which would suit him, and they had lingered, they had postponed going back to the house. So it was the old woman alone who said good-bye.

'You and Stephen must come and dine when we're settled in,' she said, as though it were still easy to command that sort of thing, as though she could any longer command anything but the devotion of poor old Fowler, doddering round on her skinny old legs. But they would like to, said Laura quickly. When she looked back over her shoulder, going down the drive, Mrs. Cranmer had gone in. The house was again a landscape without figures, its pink brick barred by the dark Venetian-blind slats of the cedars. The rooks cawed and cawed among their great untidy nests. Already it was dead, a ruin. It was almost a relief, at the lodge, to hear the living racket of Mrs. Bunt's canaries, bouncing and letting off their nerve-racking steam-whistle trills between the clean white curtains. 'Good afternoon, m'm,' called Mrs. Bunt. 'Proper summer for a change, isn't it?' She was picking currants, a little red knob of a woman with steel-rimmed glasses. Keeping the lodge wasn't what it used to be in the old days, with motors coming and going, such a turnout for a dance or a garden party, and Mr. Cranmer riding past in his mud-splashed pink on old Pericles, the good landlord, the considerate father of his people. Many was the sixpence he had given her children when they bobbed up, speechless and smiling in their pinafores. But now no more of that; Mr. Edward – or the Major, for the military title made him seem nearer to the normal Cranmer type – not caring any longer to keep that sort of thing up, even if he could, so Fowler would declare when she popped down for a cup of tea. He was very different from his father. Everything was different. All the war, the Canadian trucks rolling past, tearing up great holes in the surface of the drive, standing in rows, the nasty things, under the lime trees. And since they had left, nothing much went past Mrs. Bunt at the lodge. Mr. Vyner on his bicycle, Doctor Comstock rattling in his old Vauxhall to see Miss Sophia, businesslike, always in a hurry, listening to the old lady's heartbeats and then tearing off to a confinement five miles away, with a stop on the way to get out of the car and scramble through a briar-filled ditch to look for some Roman stones or such like. He was always asking Bunt all sorts of questions! Or there would be an occasional caller in a car, or on a bicycle even, like that Mrs. Marshall who had just gone by. But not like the old days, and never would be again, thought Mrs. Bunt, going on picking her currants. Some said good, some said not. Mrs. Bunt, for herself, could not rightly say, but she felt upset as she thought of the old days and picked the fat red currants.

XV

Victoria could be counted upon to be late home from tea with Mouse Watson. There were perhaps a couple of hours in hand, thought Laura, before her child would turn up, overheated, tired, green on the seat of her gym knickers, bleeding at each knee, and completely radiant. All the same, she must hurry. From now on it was easy going, no more hills. She sailed along easily, feeling the rush of air pleasantly on her bare legs and down the front of her dress. The lanes were narrow now, a tangle of little more than tracks along which a hay-cart could just amble and leave here a swathe on the hooks of a blackberry briar, there a rakish tuft on a slender spray of pink and paler pink dog-rose. The fingerposts had been conscientiously removed early in the war in case it should prove vital to German strategy to learn how many hedges their tanks would have to hurdle to Grimsditch or Barrow. So far they had not all been put back, so that walkers with maps slung round their necks in talc sporrans often wandered and wandered, ending up angrily in a ploughed field or somebody's sweet, dark, smoking midden. But Laura knew the way. By the broken-down cart-shed she left her bicycle, putting the bag of sweets and the chocolate in her bag, for one could ride no farther. There! The disreputable old thing sank obligingly into the nettles and the wild garlic, one wheel sticking out with an odd debauched effect of a female leg dangling. Had she brought Stuffy's lead? She began to walk up the track towards the hut.

The ground was rough, embedded in places with patches of cut stones laid together by design. Doctor Comstock had often paused here happily, his stethoscope flapping from his coat pocket, while the dying old man waited for him in the farm bedroom and the maternity nurse boiled kettles and glanced at her watch in the big new house on the hill. But the stones called out to him, like stones with voices in a legend, and he must stop his car and jump out for a few moments, a reviving glance only, before he was off and away. The Roman stones, thought Laura. They had been and gone, leaving on the land these signatures of stone, another laconic scrap of mosaic pavement in the middle of one of Mrs. Cranmer's cornfields. If the Germans had come, would any more have remained in a thousand years? Barrow Down would look the same on a hot summer day, very old, indifferent to Roman or Teuton, lonely in its green places of fern and foxglove. And now the boys from Cranmer Manor would come here and see the stones and climb the hill, chattering like the magpies which suddenly flew out, Chinese black and white, three for a wedding, four for a boy, from the woods to Laura's right.

How quiet it was! A twig cracked sharply under her feet and instantly, close at hand, a dog barked. Another answered it, and another, and – was it? Yes, without any doubt, she could recognize Stuffy's shrill voice in the middle of the pandemonium. She turned through a break in the trees into a rough field. There was the hut, in reality an old railway carriage which stood hideous and forlorn in the bleached grass, out of its native element, as though some aged locomotive had wandered and spawned here, and crawled away into the bracken to die. Four or five dogs, of vague greyhound and mongrel shape, ran forward towards Laura, barking furiously. Smoke rose from a small stick fire. Something was cooking, and garments flapped from a line, very domestic, very peaceful. Socks, a striped something, perhaps a shirt or a pyjama coat? Stuffy's voice sounded close and shrill, with no particular note of instinctive recognition, just companionably yelling with the rest. Sheets of corrugated iron at one end of the railway coach made a rough enclosure. Laura stepped up and looked in at her dog, who sat beside a bowl containing fragments of food.

'Stuffy!' she said. 'You little wretch!' But she was so glad to see the little beast, for they got caught in traps, they died down rabbit holes. As usual, Stuffy rolled over on her back and paddled the air hysterically, a hypocrite, trading shamelessly on her sex and the mushy hearts of humans, for she was not in the least sorry. Given a chance she would do it again and again, Laura well knew. But she lay there, rolling an eye, quivering ecstatically, beseeching, 'Forgive! For the last time forgive!' although somewhere in the loll of her tongue was the shadow of an impudent grin. 'You horrid little nuisance,' said Laura, stooping to pat her.

The gypsy came round the side of the hut, stepping quietly on the tussocky grass.

'Ah, you've come for her,' he said. 'I was going to wait till this evening, and if you hadn't come I'd have got on my bike and brought her along.'

'I hoped she'd come home by herself,' Laura said, 'She does sometimes.'

'Not this time,' he said, smiling. 'She was out on the spree, wasn't you, old girl? But I've been out, and I shut her up there so you'd see her if you came over. I didn't want her following me.'

'It was my own fault,' said Laura. 'I left the door open for a minute, and she must have slipped off. I thought she was in her basket.'

'She was wore out,' the man said, 'lying out there in the bracken asleep last evening, curled up like a little fox she was.

He pulled back one of the corrugated sheets, and Stuffy slipped through, cheerful and unabashed. Laura picked her up. 'Get down!' threatened the gypsy to one of the greyhounds. Which of those wagging tails, which cut of the nose, Laura wondered, would repeat itself a few weeks hence in the fat blind slugs floundering in the straw-filled wooden box? She sighed, feeling her dog's stout body warm against her side.

'She has been a great nuisance for you, I'm afraid,' she said.

'No trouble,' said the gypsy. 'Dogs do take to me, no denying it. Look what I've collected in my time! They're fond of me, I'm fond of them. Get down!' he said again, gently, to the mole-coloured greyhound.

'She's had her dinner to-day, and a good dinner yesterday,' he said to Laura.

'That's very kind of you. How much do I owe you?'

He looked at her, smiling, and she felt herself colouring. That was the wrong tone, her mother's tone. Mrs. Herriot spoke like that, crisp and kind, when she stood at the doors of the little grey cottages from which she would carry away the four-teen-year-old child in her talons. How much do I owe you, so much more delicate than a blunt How much, implying a favour done, a little contract, a bond. So often Laura had heard her mother ask that, standing holding the sitting of duck eggs or the cabbage plants or the bundle of Colonel Herriot's shirts. But here it sounded wrong, a dreadfully false note.

'Why, it's nothing,' said the man. 'She just dipped in with

the rest and enjoyed it.' He jerked his head towards the hill. 'Plenty of rabbits up there for the pot.'

She thought how funny it was that, though he had lived up here in the old railway coach and she had lived down in her house in Wealding for years, she had no idea of his name. He was anonymous himself as one of the rabbits scuttling into the fern. Even Mrs. Prout called him 'that gypsy fellow up on Barrow Down.' That gypsy fellow had been drunk again last Saturday in the Leg of Mutton, drunk as a lord, happy as a king seldom is, rolling off somehow on his bicycle with them dogs on a string. Talk about the blind leading the blind! Ernie Dummer, going out to look at an ailing sheep, had found him tumbled off his bike at the side of the road, curled up sleeping on a heap of road metal as though it were feathers, and the dogs stretched out beside him with their noses on their paws, quiet and knowing, not even growling when they heard Ernie coming. But that was all Mrs. Prout knew about him. He had never had a wife, he appeared never to have had parents. He made a bit of money helping with the harvest, mending pots and pans and the old rush-seated chairs out of the cottages, or doctoring people's sick animals. He had a wonderful way with him there. Many in Wealding would rather have the gypsy to look at their cow or tyke than Miss Stemp, the vet from Bridbury, who bustled out in her smart jodhpurs with her smart little case, like a regular doctor. But the beasts themselves seemed to have more confidence in the smell of the gypsy's hand. You saw him down in Trumper's shop, buying his rations while the dogs waited outside. You saw him in the Leg of Mutton when he came down off the hillside for his weekly spree. You never saw him in anyone's house, sitting in the armchair having a friendly chat. No, when he had made his little round, he sheered off back to the old railway coach again. When it was thick snow up on

Barrow Down and the branches of trees were snapping off sharp and brittle as barley sugar, when you couldn't set a foot outside for fear of breaking your neck, he would turn up quietly in the village, buy what he wanted, and disappear up the lonely glittering slopes once more. Mrs. Prout had to say, however, that no one spoke anything bad of him, and he had set her tabby cat's paw lovely, speaking all the time to old Tib as though she was a human.

Laura looked at him, wondering about him. For instance, how old? Difficult to tell, for he was sparely built, and this queer solitary life up here had failed to stamp him with any of the usual identification marks. He was like a letter without a postmark, no clue given as to how far or how long he had travelled. The letter was not blank, far from it, only it was written in a handwriting she did not recognize. She looked at him, slightly puzzled.

'Well, I'm awfully grateful to you,' she said. 'I can't thank you enough.'

'That's all right,' he said. He put out his hand and very tenderly scratched Stuffy's head. She tried to squirm towards him, wriggling under Laura's arm. The other dogs had wandered off, flopping down with permanent contented airs at the door of the dreadful old hut. How ugly it was, really hideous, high and dry under the great oak tree. The door stood open, and it looked very bare inside. Laura tried to picture the gypsy in there, doing little chores, frying bacon, washing out those socks which hung so domestically on the line. But the appalling little place refused to come to life as a home. It remained anonymous too, casual as a mountain hut in which climbers shelter for the night and pass on, leaving the folded blankets and the stacked firewood for the next man. You could shake a house like that off overnight, thought Laura, suddenly envious. No voices in there cry, Clean me, polish me, save me from the spider and the butterfly. No sonorous or silvery voices tick through the night, saying that time is passing, but that bricks and mortar must grind human bones to make its bread. Was it not, perhaps, extraordinary wisdom to live as casually as this, with Barrow Down for your back door and England for your front yard? She looked ahead of her and said aloud, 'Oh!' For it was higher here than she had remembered. The country was tumbled out before her like the contents of a lady's workbox, spools of green and silver and pale yellow, ribbed squares of brown stuff, a thread of crimson, a stab of silver, a round, polished gleam of mother of pearl. It was all bathed in magic light, the wonderful transforming light in which known things look suddenly new.

'Oh,' said Laura, 'how perfectly lovely it is to-day!'

'Yes, it's grand,' he said.

'You can't see Wealding from here, can you?' she asked, searching among the thick, woolly skeins of the heavy summer foliage for the familiar roofs.

'No, it lies there, behind those trees,' he said, pointing. 'You'll see it as you go higher.'

I'm not going higher, she thought, I'm going home. We do not all, she thought with an odd inward surge of exasperation, live in an appalling old shack with a pack of mongrels, my good man. Victoria will be home. Old Voller will be hobbling along to net the raspberries and set out the tender little lettuces in rows with maddening slowness. And suddenly an awful thought struck her. Had she shut the larder door when she put Miss Margesson's gooseberries on the shelf? The fish, and the cat left in the kitchen – no, already in her imagination it was eaten, and the cat was washing herself neatly, complacently, shaking out a paw daintily like a fan. Oh horrors, horrors! You cannot, Mrs. Vyner had observed earnestly in the echoing church –

you cannot, no matter what the Walk of Life, escape from its Responsibilities – she had broken holly, and seemed to bless it with a damp glance – and still retain your Self-respect. True, true, thought Laura with depression, noticing that the gypsy was far from clean, that his dark eyes might even be sly.

'But it's dreadfully lonely for you here,' she said. 'In winter especially, I should think.'

Her mother's voice again, a shade patronizing, just about to offer a blanket or a bowl of good, nourishing soup. He shook his head cheerfully.

'I don't miss company,' he said. 'The old hill gives me plenty.'

'I suppose you've got a wireless in there?' she asked, nodding towards the dreadful railway coach.

'No,' he said.

He laughed out loud, as though the idea amused him. She had to smile too, for the sound was so curiously, unusually – yes, that was the only word for it – so curiously merry. Children laughed like that, but grown ups hardly ever. Mrs. Prout's huge bosom shook, Mr. Vyner boomed and brayed, Mavis Porter's giggles floated out of the twilight at the end of the lane, irritating as the soulless shakes and whistles of Mrs. Bunt's canaries. The gypsy, however, laughed merrily, merrily, under the greenwood tree. He laughed richly, contentedly, as a fat man laughs, as though there were layers of jolly fat on his spiritual bones. For actually he was so thin, his old trousers were too big for him, and they were tied round his waist with a bit of string.

'I'm not the one for a wireless,' he said.

She had still a half-irritated wish to trap him somehow, to bring him down into the native reservation with the rest of them. For we all have to do it. We stand in queues, shuffling our feet, waiting for the wrath of Mr. Kellett to descend like icy, dirty water on our meek heads. We put on our bowler hats and journey to London, though the day calls for us to live like gods. We get into the bus, the door clicks like a mousetrap, and it rolls forward towards Miss Grant and the hot classroom, Miss Trasker and 'Water Lily Elves' and attention to the slurs. We conform, we conform, all of us. Why should anybody escape?

'But sometimes you come down into the village,' she said.

'When I want to buy something to eat or something to drink,' he said.

He laughed again. Somehow he knew that she knew he had wobbled off his bike and slept on the heap of road metal.

'Mr. Marshall wants someone to do a bit of gardening,' she said suddenly. 'Do you garden? Would you be able to come some evenings?'

'Well, I don't know,' he said. 'Maybe I'll call round one night and take a look at the job. Yes, maybe I'll come along with the dogs one night and talk to Mr. Marshall.'

But he wouldn't come. She knew that perfectly well.

'Good-bye,' she said, 'and thanks again for looking after my dog.'

'Are you going up to the top?' he asked. 'Seems a pity, as you're so near. It's wonderful fine up there to-day.'

'No, I must go home,' Laura said. 'I've left my bicycle down at the bottom of the track.'

'Good day then,' he said.

She turned and walked out of the clearing. He whistled to the dogs to stop them following her. When she got on the other side of the trees, she set Stuffy down and hitched the lead on to her collar. Now, she thought, quickly home to the fish, the cat, to Victoria, to the domestic cave. But she stood quite still, looking up the track where it twisted higher between the sunken banks and the smooth roots of trees which seemed to splay and float in the surf of last year's leaves, like the roots of seaweed which would float up, up, into the lighter green wash far above. Perhaps she might go to the top after all, she thought. Why not? In the bus that morning she had envied the young man in the blue shirt for his infernal masculine nonchalance, shaking his shoulders as he adjusted the straps of his knapsack, striding away from them all, the hot women, the frightful shopping-baskets, swinging calmly off to climb Barrow Down. It was suddenly immensely important that she, too, should climb Barrow Down. There was so seldom the time or the opportunity to step even so slightly out of the common round, the horribly trivial task. She looked over her shoulder to see if the gypsy had followed and was watching her through the trees. But there was not a sound, not a sign. The rough clearing and the nasty little cabin might have been a dream.

'Come along,' she said to Stuffy, giving a little pull to the lead, for her dog seemed to be holding back, pulling back towards the railway coach and the gypsy.

They began to climb the hill.

XVI

At the top, a slight breeze fanned her hot face. Down below it had seemed that there was not a breath of air, the heavy trees were billowing feather-beds in which even the birds were languidly silent. But up here there was a hilltop freshness which just stirred the tops of the few gaunt trees with which Barrow Down was crowned. Some said the clump was something to do with Druids; others, that it had been planted by the whim of a bygone Cranmer. It made, at any rate, a convenient shelter for picnic parties and their wavering spirit-lamps. To-day there were no picnic parties. Half-way up, Laura and Stuffy, by mutual consent, had stopped and disentangled themselves from one another. After all, thought Laura, stooping to unhook the lead, it is pretty safe to say that there will be nobody up here. On Sundays there were always walkers with ash sticks and dogs, and at least one stout, panting woman toiling good humouredly to the top with a grey little man in a town Sunday suit. On Sundays, too, came the riders from the livery stables in Bridway, bouncing young women in open-necked shirts, young men whose sleek pasted hair would lift in the wind as they lolloped along on the knowing old hacks. But on a weekday it would be a surprise to meet anybody except, perhaps, an occasional shepherd. So you should be all right, said Laura to Stuffy, who had been apparently working herself towards an apoplexy. But directly she was released, she ran busily along, showing no inclination to double back to the gypsy's greyhounds. This unexpected bonus of a walk was delightful. Love was forgotten. She ran, she sniffed, she barked furiously on the track of squirrels who lightly, scornfully, shinned up the masts like cabin boys.

And Laura had been right. They had Barrow Down to themselves except for an army of rabbits who leapt in the air and vanished. Some sheep appeared by the dewpond, saw Stuffy, and began running with the tucked-down chins, the braced behinds, and rapid little steps of elderly ladies trying to catch a bus. Laura followed in the same direction. She felt that she would die if she did not rest for a moment, she was so sticky and out of breath. Her heart was pounding. She must be in terribly bad training! When she had walked half-way round the Barrow clump, she threw herself down on the grass and stared up at the sky. It was softly, deeply blue, paler than at midday, and the larks singing invisibly high up in it threw down their eerie, other-world thread of song to Laura lying on her back among the little milky blue and pink flowers. The ground beneath her seemed just faintly to rock and sway in a lovely, sleepy movement. It shook with a mighty, gusty roaring, the pounding of Stuffy's paws and her panting as she approached and tried affectionately to lie down on Laura's face.

'Go away,' said Laura.

She sat up, rolling Stuffy over with one hand while with the other she pushed the damp hair up from her neck. Ah, how delicious! She sighed, and for the first time dropped her gaze into the great humming bowl of England which lay at her feet. It startled her by being so much vaster than she remembered.

For it was years since she had climbed up here – no, not since the first summer of the war. Then some woman friend had been staying with her, Sonia Peel it was, and they had packed tea and brought it up on Barrow Down as a little celebration of Mark Peel's sixth birthday. Stephen was in camp up in Yorkshire, Sonia's husband was on a destroyer somewhere or other, the wireless went on quietly and reasonably saying awful things every evening when they sat in the somehow stillborn, depressing cosiness of two women having a sherry together. It was not altogether for Mark that they made the little effort of the picnic party. Cutting the bread, spreading the jam, screwing up the thermos flask and the children's milk bottle were calming ritual gestures, promising that the everyday world would continue. The pink and white birthday cake, elegantly fluted – for there was still a cook in Laura's kitchen – was normal and reassuring as a cheerful known face. But as they lit the candles, somewhat unsuccessfully, among the paper bags and the ants up on Barrow Down, Laura had suddenly sat back on her heels and said, Isn't it –? and it was, unmistakably, a distant siren moaning from the coast. Then Bridbury's siren had spoken, and before anyone had bitten into the birthday icing the sky was chattering with machine-gun fire, high, seemingly harmless, until down came the planes, turning, groaning, bellowing in their agony as the black smoke puffed out. One – two – three, shouted Victoria. Poor Sonia Peel, who was expecting another baby, sat like a large white tent, a hideously visible target exposed on the top of Barrow Down. The noise died away. After a pause the sirens breathed a gentler, one-syllable song. They gathered up sandwich papers and brushed away crumbs. *What* a nice birthday, said Mark.

So on that occasion Laura could not remember giving much attention to the view, and before the war, somehow, she and

Stephen had little time to climb up to Barrow Down. It loomed over them always, it was the background of their days. But scramble up to it – ah no, very seldom. They knew that it was there and that the view from the top was the best, people said, in three counties. Sometimes they walked an energetic week-end guest up there. God, to have *this* at your door! the guests would exclaim, scooping the wonderful air into their fogbound lungs, planting their shiny city brogues firmly on the moss and thinking vaguely of the Druids, of Drake, of this precious stone set in a silver sea, of the imminent Sunday roast beef and Yorkshire pudding. To which the Marshalls would make a modest murmur and avoid catching each other's eye. For how often did they make the effort? In the week-ends there were always people coming, there was tennis, Stephen was shooting at Cranmer. And since the war had ended, Laura thought, they were still more bound to the tyrant house, she to the kitchen, Stephen, when he was home, to the lawn mower and the wood-pile, the dirty boots and the devilish bindweed. When had they been up here last together, simply together? She could not remember.

However, here she was, she thought in some surprise. Because she had heard the telephone and run in from the garden, leaving the door open, because Stuffy had slipped off to a light-of-love by hole in the hedge, and field track, and mysterious, beckoning scent in the damp ditch – here she was. Her day which had begun so prosaically in hot Bridbury, dangling a limp, resigned basket outside Rosemary's Tea Shoppe, had landed her on top of the lonely hill. Ah Stuffy, what a good turn you really did me, she thought, gently tick-ling the stout stomach of her dog, a sagging pinkish carpet-bag worn shapeless with careless maternity. You and Mrs. Porter, she thought, what a pair of you. Easy come, easy go, does it matter who, a greyhound or a fat corporal named Tuck, a black mongrel or a thin Canadian? And really, said Stuffy's rolling eye, it does not matter, not in the least. Love beamed from Stuffy's eye and from her panting mouth, love unselective, uncritical, bestowing its favours without calculation. Annabel Trumper would marry Mr. Rudge, and An excellent thing, Mrs. Cranmer had pronounced it. But Live lightly, preached Stuffy and Mrs. Porter as they frisked in the bracken. Live lightly, the gypsy had said without a word as he stood looking at her outside the awful little shack, looking at the grey-haired Wealding lady who had come fussily, leash in hand and tip in purse, searching for her dog.

It is all very well, thought Laura, fretfully, but what can I do? I cannot cut and run like Stuffy away from the dull basket and the all too familiar bowl. I am a perfectly happy married woman, simply getting a little greyer, duller, more tired than I should be getting, because my easier sort of life has come to an end. Neither can I drag Victoria and Stephen to live in an old railway carriage planted on a hillside. Unfortunately we are all slaves of the turned-back fresh linen, the polished wood reflecting the civilized candlelight, the hot water running into the shining bath. No, she thought, there was nothing to be done. Beside her, Stuffy suddenly ceased to pant, withdrawing her tongue and closing her jaw with a slight click, as though a switch had been turned off. Closing her eyes, pillowing her dusty head, she slept, virtuous, undreaming. So much wiser than humans, who would excuse or accuse or hate somebody, she had loved and been lost. Found again, full of happiness at regaining Laura, she sighed, stretched out on the grass, and slept deeply. The pinkish carpet-bag bulged and collapsed peacefully, soothingly, with her breathing.

I wish, thought Laura, that Stephen were here, looking at

the view beside me. If he were here, she would say to him – what would she say? She did not know, but there was something to be said, something which was often on the tip of her tongue but which eluded her in the rushed moments at breakfast, the evenings when he was tired and she was tired. But if he were here beside her, stretched out on the grass looking at England, she might think of it. She sat clasping her hands together round her knees, her scratched and reddened left hand uppermost, on which the thin gold wedding ring looked surprised and bright. Over there was the sea, a misty streak sharply outlined by a broad ribbon of white light. The cold English sea – she followed it in her imagination, all blue for once to-day, lapping quietly round the coast, sucking the concrete blocks which had been going to play Canute to the invader, drawing a wrinkle of silk over the long sands where pink-toed children ran brandishing starfish by a rough pink ray, washing a deeper, more southern purple and indigo round the black rocks of St. Pol, then up the melancholy gull-haunted estuaries and past the ruined castle on the grey point, round the farthest lonely islands with the names like wild poetry, running up in gentle wavelets on shingle above which the Regency houses in need of paint turned peeling faces towards the great land mass of Europe, sighing against the chalk cliffs, and finally tying its girdle round the island's green waist with that knot of shining broad ribbon. There was a mysterious virtue in the sight of the misty streak. To-morrow, Laura promised herself, she and Victoria would be there, eating their sandwiches among the sand dunes. Why had they not done it to-day? Why, for that matter, had she not taken the time to climb the hill and look at the view all these years? Barrow Down was at her door, it was too idiotic, but there she was all the time, down in her house in Wealding, struggling to keep up a way of life which had really ended. Ah, fool, she thought.

Foolish matron sitting beside that other wiser matron, the snoring Stuffy, who simply gambolled off to find what she wanted beneath the broad blue sky of this fine summer day.

She sat looking at the view. It drew the eye on to distant hills, to aerial villages, to unsubstantial, heavenly wraiths of towns which flashed a sudden signal from a golden window. If Stephen were here, he would identify them all, for he was a methodical man, he loved maps, names, and populations, the height of this and the depth of that. But Laura looked vaguely at the spirit shapes of towns which could not possibly be urban communities containing cinemas and Wesleyan chapels and shops where the shopping women stood, dangling their limp, resigned baskets. The little breeze fanned her cheek, the distant golden window – or was it the windscreen of a car? – flashed again. And suddenly she thought that she would speak to Stephen this evening, she would suggest that they might go away together for a little holiday. Since he had come home from the war they had never been away alone together. Victoria, like the poor, was always with them, no longer conveniently removed by stout Nannie and produced again in the evening, clean and delicious in her little blue dressing-gown with the pink rabbit on the pocket. He picked his way, poor Stephen, through a house littered with the navy-blue pools of a little girl's gym knickers, lying still warm on the floor where Victoria had hopped out of them. Hideous contraptions of wire glittered on the bathroom shelf, seeming to grin at him when he went in to shave in the morning. Sorry! Victoria would say airily, palming the thing into her mouth and running down to practise. One, two, three, galumphed the infernal Water Lily Elves, while Stephen stood shaving, listening, visibly suffering. He would have liked a son, Laura knew that. He loved Victoria, but he would have liked a boy; he bent to knock out his pipe in the evenings after the fiendish wireless had said its say, and sometimes, quite unconsciously, he sighed deeply. Perhaps, like Miss Margesson, in a queer sort of way he even missed the war, sitting there surrounded by his female household, knocking out his pipe. Ah, but we used to have such fun together, thought Laura in amazement. Walking in those great chestnut forests, and returning to eat the trout and the wild strawberries and to talk to the fat old man, pink as a fat powdered baby in his chef's apron and shirt sleeves. Sitting eating those delicious little rum cakes while the stout piano and the thin violin shook the life out of Verdi, and the serious men bent over the chess board, and flies settled on the newspapers in the racks. And little adventures, even, happening to them all the time. Being lost on mountains, stranded in god-forsaken little villages smelling of snow and cowdung, but everything coming out right in the end, with hot drinks and a fire, a clean little wooden room like the inside of a cigar box, a great deal of laughter and always somebody enchanting to talk to, a woodcutter or a priest or the jolly woman making an omelette for them. But suddenly there was no more fun, there were no more adventures, George Porter's blue eyes regarded a sofa, Stephen bent and knocked out his pipe, sighing deeply. If they could be quiet together for a little while, with a hill to walk on and a sea to swim in, might not something come back? For we are so lucky, so enormously lucky, thought Laura. Up here, in this clear rarefied light, their luck seemed immense. They were alive, they were all together. Sonia Peel, who had sat here like a large white tent while the planes clanged overhead, was now a widow. Desmond Peel had never seen the new baby. The oily waters had closed over Jim Trumper's red head. Laura's friends had left their husbands for someone else, or their husbands had left them for someone else. But here they were, the Marshalls, still a unit, still making sense in a world which every day seemed to signify less. Their wonderful, stupendous luck, thought Laura. Now that she had a free moment in which to stand back and look at it, it struck her as stupendous. She began to plan. She would ask her mother to stay on, after the expedition to Mr. Briggs in Wimpole Street, and look after Victoria for a week or two. The house, she thought, feeling light-hearted already, could go to pot – absolutely to pot! Mrs. Herriot and Mrs. Prout would, she knew, conduct an embittered war to the death until her return, pitting the sniff delicate against the sniff insolent, pursuing Laura with endless dispatches from the battlefront of plaintive, voluminous letters and cryptic postcards, written with squared elbows at the Prout kitchen table. But let them fight, she did not care. It was as simple as that. Aunt Vi could stop and look after her father in St. Pol. He would grumble, but as long as the indispensable female figure was there behind the tea-cosy he would not really mind. The hens, the ducks, the fine shades of the weekly shopping which had to be arranged so that she was calm and pleasant with Mr. Kellett, gay and rallying with Mr. Tubbs, the butcher – would her mother manage it all? But the idea had come to her, she refused to waver or be discouraged. Let them all fight, she thought, nothing matters but Stephen. And now I must go home, for it is certainly getting late.

She did not stir. The golden eye blinked again, far out in the warm haze. Yes, it was a car, for it was moving. She watched it half-sleepily, listening to the hum floating up from the great bowl. It was the summer voice of England, seeming to say in the rattle of the hay-carts, the swish of the blades laying sorrel and clover in swathes, the murmur and buzz of the uncut fields, the men's deep voices calling peacefully across the dead quiet, We are at peace. An aeroplane flew south, trundling along, flashing a silver blink to the gold blink below, and Laura watched it go as idly as she had watched the car crawl and dip along the unknown road. Planes were no longer something to glance up at warily. The long nightmare was over, the land sang its peaceful song. Thank God, thought Laura again as she had thought in the bus while the young man in the blue shirt read his map, but this time the feeling of thankfulness was so overwhelming that the view suddenly misted, gathered, and hung shining, and she rummaged in her bag for her handkerchief. Heavens knows, she thought sarcastically, the fact should have registered before, she had had occasions in plenty to get her weeping done with official sanction. The fireworks had thrown their nests of squirming gold and silver caterpillars high in the air, the bonfires had crackled on the green and up here on Barrow Down. For a whole week, rich boozy brass voices had gone on beseeching everybody to roll out the barrel, assuring the silent woods and fields that there would always be an England. The young women had whisked their best dresses at a Victory ball, the young children had been gorged into fretfulness at a Victory tea, by Saturday victory was sour on everyone's tongue, as cold as the ashes of the bonfires. Let us give thanks, Mr. Vyner said, very simple, very quiet, when the handful of the faithful bowed their tired knees before God. But never, even then, had Laura felt quite this rush of overwhelming thankfulness, so that the land swam and misted and danced before her. She had had to lose a dog and climb a hill, a year later, to realize what it would have meant if England had lost. We are at peace, we still stand, we will stand when you are dust, sang the humming land in the summer evening.

But would it last, this calm and lovely pause, this beautiful weather? Her eyes flew in alarm to the western sky, where there was a bank of something, hardly threatening yet, a coppery tinge only. Was it thunder? It had been so hot all day. There's thunder about, a voice had said in the stifling bus this morning, calm, stating a positive fact, not displeased with the idea that an English summer was an eccentric. Ah no, Laura protested, the weather could not possibly break now, just as she was enjoying the peace and calm, just as she and Victoria were going to pack their sandwiches and go to the sea. 'It mustn't break,' she said aloud, so firmly that the pinkish carpet-bag heaved and Stuffy reared an inquiring head, looking round for the enemy. Keep away, she said to the sultry tinge in the fair sky. For we want some fine days, everyone says so. What we want, they said, leaning on the spade or across the shopping-baskets in the crowded bus, is a nice long spell of fine weather. Oh, I want it for Victoria to-morrow, Laura thought. 'It isn't anything, it's all right,' she said to Stuffy, who was growling. She lay back again on the grass for a moment, only a moment, pressing her cheek against the milky little flowers as she looked sideways, through half-closed eyes, down into the singing bowl. It must last for Victoria, the beautiful weather. And again the earth beneath her seemed to give its delicious half-sway. I want a good deal for Victoria, she thought drowsily, but not the same things that my mother wanted for me. Nothing better than this. A quiet evening, a house and a child in the valley, time to climb a hill by herself. But it is only possible, she thought confusedly, if we are left alone, if the good weather lasts. How the bowl hummed with all its voices, sleepy as crickets in the grass! Be not afeared, Mrs. Cranmer had said long, long ago, the isle is full of noises. How it hummed, her dear isle. And suddenly the hum was music, Mrs. Vyner's music, swelling, dying away, seeming about to state something which Laura would never forget in the split second before her eyelids drooped, her eyelids sealed. Mrs. Vyner's music swelled out of the air, but enormously stronger, fortified by a million strings.

She could see through her flickering lashes the wing-like movement of all the arms beating up and down, drawing the bows up and down across the glittering air – or were they really some large white birds, pigeons, seagulls, flapping slowly across the blue? But the music went on, the whole world was playing it now, she struggled to keep awake and hear it, the answer. 'If only the weather doesn't break,' she said to Stephen, who was sitting listening beside her. The earth rocked once, twice, Mrs. Vyner's piano reared up and yawned, the crickets played a piercingly sweet passage close to her ear.

She slept.

XVII

Victoria Marshall approached her home. Laura's guess had been accurate. She was green on the seat and dirty on the knees, and she had also torn her blouse and lost a hair-ribbon. She was extremely happy. In her hand joggled the music case, grown portly with a package containing cream cheese which Mrs. Watson at the last moment had crammed down between 'Water Lily Elves' and 'Little Gavotte.' 'Daddy will enjoy it for his tea to-night,' Mrs. Watson had said. 'They don't have tea, they have sort of dinner,' Victoria had said gloomily, 'but I'm sure he'll enjoy it all the same.' Her own stomach felt tight and comfortable as a drum. Tea at the Watsons' was a major event. Everyone came and sat down comfortably round the big table in the kitchen, Mouse, her two elder sisters, Maud, the chicken girl, and Mr. Watson if he was home. 'Eat up now,' Mrs. Watson urged, piling buttery potato cakes on Victoria's plate, and there was more butter on the table, sometimes a little dish of cream as well, and a dark fruity cake, and saffron buns which melted in the mouth. Victoria, overeating with scientific greed, had thought enviously of Mr. Watson's Jersey cows even now standing in their stalls waiting to be milked, pretty as Siamese cats, their moist brown noses shining. Why, oh why, hadn't her father seen fit to own a farm? There sat Mouse, hardly eating a thing, used to it. 'Yes, please,' said Victoria to a third slice, although the girdle of her gym tunic warned her. And then later on, Mouse had told her, at about ten o'clock they all sat down to another tea! That was the way to live, thought Victoria. No nonsense about lugging everything into the dining-room or having the silver teapot in the drawing-room. Last winter, when it was so cold, they had tried eating in the kitchen at home, but it did not work. Her mother was always distractedly peering under the tablecloth for the egg whisk, or sitting down just as something boiled over on the stove. Damn! said her father, pushing his chair back and knocking into the dresser. They were not happy, they could not settle, they had the distrait air of cats whose feet had not been buttered. Back they all had to go into the freezing higher air of the dining-room. And her mother's cakes, thought Victoria sadly as she took another fruity, spicy mouthful, were apt to be discouraged things, sagging limply, or developing huge cracks across craggy peaks which seemed to have been blackened by some devouring fire. Not that it was her fault, Victoria suddenly added in loving reflection, for Laura looked so awfully sad, looking mournfully down at the funny black cake. It was the oven. Laura said that many times. That old beast of an oven, darling, and she could make it sound quite funny, and they laughed over the cake which was not really bad when you had finished picking out all the charred haddock's eyes of sultanas.

Victoria leant back, the girdle pleasantly constricted. It was nice in the Watsons' kitchen. No wonder they preferred to sit here always rather than in the front parlour, a glacial apartment dominated by an upright rosewood piano, a fan of pleated pink paper ironically imitating flames in the glistening grate, and many photographs of wedding groups and Mr. Watson's prize cattle, looking not so very different. Bob's photograph was also there, in the place of honour on the piano top under the plumes of dried pampas grass. Bob had been killed in the war, and Victoria thought it was a shame that he had been banished to the front parlour, past which even the animals, the cat and the old terrier, sheered in a hurry as they made for the fire and the shabby rag hearth-rug. To-day, of course, the fire was not so comforting. The door stood open into the cool flagged scullery, every window was wide, Mrs. Watson's forehead was flushed and shining. 'Thunder about,' said Maud, the chicken girl, lifting an arm as though it were a wing, and she a hen herself, and slowly, luxuriously scratching her shoulder. 'Oh, why ever didn't we lay tea out under the apple tree?' sighed the eldest daughter, blooming Ada. She frowned, she crumbled cake daintily, a line appeared in her white forehead. Did she, Victoria wondered, wish that they were sitting in the front parlour among the photographs? Perhaps she did. She was engaged to be married to Ronnie, a doctor who had met her when she was nursing. Now he was out of the Army, Ada would be a doctor's wife far from Wealding, and she thought all the time, Mouse reported, of crochet table-mats and drawing-room suites. They would be married next month by Mr. Vyner, Mouse and Pat in pale blue, the bridegroom's little nephew Duncan as a sweet little sailor boy. Victoria gazed hungrily at the interesting bride.

'The old lady,' they were saying. Mrs. Watson leant back, recalling comfortably, 'I remember going up to Cranmer once, a sale of work or something – or maybe a flower show? I forget. But oh, the rooms, and the cabinets full of stuff! Such pictures!'

'Nobody's got time nowadays to look after a place like that,' said Maud.

'I wish she'd have an auction there,' said the bride. 'Ronnie and I wouldn't mind buying some of her things. I could do with a cabinet, a nice cabinet.'

'Come on,' Mouse said in a low voice to Victoria, and off they went.

They scuffled about for a while in the granary and Victoria tore her blouse on a nail. Zip! The tear ran up her arm like a mouse. Then they went to look at the bull, huge, melancholy, a ring through his pink nose and a frizzled puff of white wool on his vast forehead. Victoria stood very still, staring, fascinated. How perfectly huge, how sad! 'Catch,' said Mouse, digging her in the ribs, and they tore away, squealing, kicking up their heels, rolling in the orchard grass. Exhausted, they lay there and told each other stories. Victoria liked the way Mouse spoke, rolling, a little slurred in some of the sounds. What a dreadful accent that friend of Victoria's has! she had overheard her grandmother say one day when Mouse had come to tea and Mrs. Herriot was staying with them. It's only Wealding, her mother replied – Victoria was outside the kitchen where the two of them were working, covering jam pots. I rather like it, her mother had said, and Victoria, guilty but interested, heard the snap of an elastic band going round another jar of goose-berry jam. I do *not*, said her grandmother decisively, Victoria will be picking it up next, and her nice little voice will be spoilt. Everything so dreadfully *mixed* now, Victoria heard her grandmother mourning rather puzzlingly as she edged out of hearing. For half an hour she was self-conscious about her nice little voice. She was a frail flower. Then she forgot all about it until this minute. Dreadful accent, indeed! What rot they talked!

'I must go,' she sighed regretfully, a couple of hours or so later. And here she was, plodding home, tired, extremely happy. She envied Mouse, lucky Mouse, daughter of a father who had been glimpsed coming out of the big milking-shed, a stout, red-faced man, genial monarch of all those dark-eyed Jerseys and the impossible great rock of a bull with his frizzed topknot. How different, Victoria could not help thinking, from her own father. For a moment or two she tried in a discouraged way to graft geniality on to Stephen, who refused, who had shouted only this morning, What the hell is this beastly thing? as though he had found a cockroach in the bathroom instead of merely her plate. Sorry, she had said airily, but he had continued ungenial, grumbling all through breakfast to her mother about the garden, which anybody could see was perfectly all right. Of course she loved him, as one always loved one's father, easily, without noticing, like breathing. But it had not been too awful, all the same, while he was away. There were often other children staying in the house, the Peels, the Barkers, John and Sally Chadwick, and sometimes one of the mothers could manage the old beast of an oven quite skilfully. Food was queer, but interesting. Her mother and the other mothers ate on trays, the house got untidier and untidier. Now and then a bomb fell in Wealding, and then they would be rushed downstairs and tucked up on the sofa, and fed chocolates with no mention made of cleaning teeth afterwards. When she and her mother were quite alone it was even more fun. For there were different ways of loving people, some easily like breathing, others with more pain, more delicious pressure in the chest. On winter nights the house was their primitive shelter, their cave. They hung up the blackout and sat by the fire together, playing cards. In the summer they sometimes cut sandwiches and took the bus to the sea. To the sea! thought Victoria, stopping dead in the lane and sniffing the air as though she could smell the salt, the beautiful fishy stink of the sea purses and dried bits of weed and rotting backbones in which Stuffy loved to roll at the foot of the sand dunes. Ah, what bliss! Her mother could be so funny, funnier than anyone Victoria knew. Sitting cross-legged in her bathing-suit, she waved a lettuce leaf and suddenly something happened to her face, her upper lip lengthened, her eyes became round and mournful, and there was Miss Grant, twitching and nibbling. Victoria rolled and choked with laughter. Or she would be Mrs. Prout, or even old Voller squeaking away about the mice eating the pea seeds. But they had not been to the sea for ages. Now that her father was home, her mother always seemed to be standing by the stove, stirring things, and frowning at the book in her hand. Victoria's bedtime, which had been an elastic affair, returned to a legal appointed hour. Lying in bed, she could hear them talking downstairs, together in the cave. On summer evenings they came out into the garden, and Victoria, peeping through the curtains drawn to keep out the heartless sunlight, would see them strolling away, her father saying Look! at something on the lawn, perhaps the poor daisies, and her mother answering I know, and standing there, sniffing a crushed leaf of verbena, before slipping a hand through her father's arm and strolling off, the tall pair of them. Everything was different, everything, thought Victoria. But when she grew up, she would work on a farm, whatever they said behind the glass partition. She swung the music case high in the air and brought it down with a thump.

There was a short cut across a field and through the churchyard. The iron gate clanged, and there she was among all the dead people. In this new part of the graveyard, there were rows of green tin cornets and jam jars, stuffed with tight bunches of roses and Canterbury bells, and the grass was neatly trimmed, and the gravel was weedless, as though people were trying to soften the stern mystery and deny the pitiless rains with the homy touches of flowers and a snug turf eiderdown. The graves had almost a convalescent look. At any moment Hannah, wife of William, and Nathaniel, departed this life September 1938, might sit up, push back the bouquets, and declare themselves a good deal better. Farther on, the possessive love of the living had long ago died too, and the long grass and moon daisies waved round the anonymous wedded tombstones, heeling gently over together under the confetti of the Scotch briar petals. This part was really much nicer, thought Victoria.

To-day there was a new mound of reddish-yellow, raw-looking earth. Somebody had just been buried, for the flowers were perfectly fresh. Victoria went up the path to take a peep and read some of the cards. 'Our darling Mother, from Aggie and Flo,' 'With deep sympathy, Mr. and Mrs. Albert Smith' – ah, how funny, as though it were Christmas! She screwed up her eyes tightly and held her breath, to see how it would be to be dead. Ugh! It was horrid! She opened them again extremely wide, and started walking away very quickly. But at the church door she could not resist a peep inside. The empty church had the fascination of the shop seen through a window on early-closing day, its stands bare, its busy life arrested. Nobody was in the church, stealthy old Nobody, mouthing from the pulpit, lurking in the folds of the red plush curtain behind which Mr. Vyner kept his surplice. Stepping in here, after the warmth and buzz outside, was like stepping under the sea. At the far end of the dim green grotto, where angels or mermaids swam with their golden hair flowing, the gold cross shone steadily. There, thought Victoria, Ada will kneel, followed by Mouse in pale-blue silk with sweet peas, and the little sailor boy nephew. She felt very solemn. But what was that dreadful deep ticking sound, slow and weighty, as though the heart of the church was beating away all the time? She jumped, glancing nervously over her shoulder. Only the clock! All the same, she tiptoed out very fast, closing the wire grille carefully after her, and not slackening her pace until she was through the lych-gate.

There were plenty of things to tell her mother. She began to rehearse them to herself as she walked up the hill towards the house. The day at school, the wonderful tuck-in at the Watsons', the cream cheese produced nonchalantly, for climax, out of the music case. And did Laura know that there were oranges to-day in Bridbury? Half the girls had come boasting of oranges in the sideboard dish at home, but her mother was so vague, Victoria reflected, that she was apt to let these things slip if you did not warn her. A regular dreamer, your ma, Mrs. Prout had said one day, suddenly looking at her in a flatteringly grown-up, confidential way as she scraped out a spoilt something or other from a pie dish. And even Victoria could tell that her mother was different from cheery, pretty Mrs. Bellamy, whose children were always so disgustingly neat and clean, or from fat Mrs. Watson, whose kitchen smelt of hot, spicy goodness. Yes, she was dreadfully vague! But how one loved her, so that it often became pleasurable pressure somewhere in the chest. And Victoria began to run, the strands of her loosened pigtail flopping. Here was her gate, her familiar weedy gravel. She came in with a skip, noticing a tricycle pushed just inside the garage doors – so old Voller was here. Bursting with the burden of all she had to say, Victoria skipped up to the front door. It was locked. So was the back door, where the cat, plaintively waiting, greeted her with rapture. But there was always a spare key hidden under a flower pot, which thieves were supposed not to lift, and Victoria let herself in, throwing down the music case, crying 'Mummy!' She ran through the kitchen, along the passage, into the hall, expecting at any moment to hear Laura's voice answering Hallo, darling, from upstairs somewhere, perhaps from the depths of a cupboard where she was sitting surrounded by their old clothes, making one of her occasional over-ambitious raids of tidying up.

Silence. Nobody answered, frightening old Nobody, who had followed her back from church and now was taking possession of the empty rooms where a little clock ticked loudly and a bee buzzed wearily, wearily, against the glass. Laura was always there waiting, calling Hallo, darling! Now there was old Nobody. Very slowly, Victoria walked over to the hall table and put down her music case.

XVIII

Stephen Marshall let himself down into the seat of his car, outside Ashton station, with a grunt of relief. He threw his hat and the evening paper over his shoulder on to the back seat. The other men went by, finding their cars in the park. Some of them lived in Ashton itself, a horrible hole, a nice old town which had been ruined by a cancer of stock-brokers' desirable residences, of Tudor cafés and Georgian banks and Assyrian picture palaces, so that now its only virtue was that you could leave it by fast train for London every half-hour. A few of the men travelled up and down daily from homes in Bridbury; two or three, like Stephen and Hector Bellamy, came from even further afield. There went Bellamy now, thought Stephen, pressing the self-starter. A remarkably handsome fellow, owning a pretty wife and a well-kept house and garden, wearing the right sort of tie, laughing on the right easy, friendly note, confound him. He had done extremely well in the war, and now here he was, planting his glossy shoes so confidently on the dusty ground, looking round complacently with his slightly prominent blue eyes as though he fully intended to do extremely well in the peace too. Every morning they travelled up in the same carriage, and Bellamy unfolded his copy of The

Times, shook it out, and glanced along the headlines, faintly smiling, thoughtfully stroking his small clipped moustache, the picture of a well-tubbed, well-shaven, well-breakfasted man who was at peace with all the world. Here I am again, thank God, on the good old 8.47, Bellamy seemed to be confiding to his moustache. This is what I missed all these years, this is what I dreamt about. And when the train ran into the dirty, echoing station, Bellamy would fish his bowler hat out of the rack and put it on his head, settling it deeply on his forehead as though it were a crown. He would fold *The Times* neatly under his arm, square his shoulders, shoot an impatient blue glance over the heads of the lesser men getting off the train in front of him, and off he would go to conquer London. Until this moment it had not occurred to Stephen that he envied Bellamy. To be so absolutely sure that you had got what you wanted, to have held tightly on to something for so long, and to find it waiting for you unflawed! Stephen began to edge out of the car park, and Bellamy, two cars away, raised his hand and called, 'So long, old man.' So long indeed, thought Stephen, braking to let one of the station taxis get past. Twenty years long, by his count. Barring another major interruption, he could think of no reason why he should not be travelling up on the 8.47, watching Bellamy sing his silent *Te Deum* to his moustache, for the next twenty years or so. The prospect filled him with two things – first, with dreadful gloom, and, second, with surprise that he had done it for so many years already, but had only, this first summer of the peace, realized that the prospect filled him with dreadful gloom. There was not a thing to be done about it. But sometimes in the night – he was a poor sleeper – he would lie there imagining the most ridiculous things, seeing them selling the house, going abroad somewhere – Canada, Rhodesia, New Zealand? – seeing Laura in a print dress picking extraordinary blue and flame-pink trumpet-shaped flowers from a white picket fence, seeing a lot of young horses in a big paddock, and beyond them an immense stretch of lovely rolling grey country without a single smudge of smoke in the sky, and himself with an axe, cutting down something in the background. It was all a dream, blurred, changing shape and colour, and all the time he knew that it wasn't true, it would never be so. He would never leave England. He loved it too much. He would go on sitting opposite Hector Bellamy on the 8.47, and when it happened over again next time, there he would be, trapped, waiting to be overtaken by the final catastrophe which he had not had the wits to dodge. For it would remain just an idea to play with. Sometimes the house was white, sometimes it was built of wood, sometimes it was surrounded by orange groves watered by streams of melting snow running down from the mountains, and sometimes there was nothing but forests in which he would learn to watch the birds, like Edward Cranmer. But it did not matter. It was all just nonsense, for he would never leave England. He knew that perfectly well.

The traffic lights held him up in the High Street. The shops were shut, and in the beautiful summer evening light, without the crowds of hot women bumping each other off the pavements with their shopping-baskets, the street had acquired a sort of dignity, flowing slightly uphill towards the town's chief glory, the really superb town hall. There it stood, a logical statement in stone among the incoherence which men had created round it, and in the niche under the great clock stood Queen Anne, holding the orb and sceptre, staring with an expression of pouting disapproval at the red and golden temple of Woolworth's. For some reason – a charter, a church, a charity – she was connected with Ashton, and there she stood, the old girl, a magnificent ship of state in her gilded stone robes, curled and puffed and jewelled, glaring out at the town, as well she might. Sham and gimcrackeries flowed right up to her feet, dishonest buildings crowded in on her, the shop windows paraded the tawdry and unreal right up to the plate-glass portals of the picture palace, where people were going in now out of the beautiful summer evening to witness the unreal pursue the tawdry across the dark screen and possess them with one final burst of ecstasy, one last delirious spasm of Rachmaninoff played by a potted symphony orchestra. Better in my day, in spite of the pox, Queen Anne appeared to be saying, staring sardonically out of her little gilded dog kennel. What a mess of a street, what a mess we have made of the whole thing, thought Stephen, but somehow he rather liked its typical English muddle and laziness this evening. He waited for the lights to go yellow, his hand ready on the gear lever. Two young girls went along on the pavement, off to meet their boys, probably at the Ashton Lido, for towels and bathing-suits hung in their hands. He watched them idly. Were they fifteen or nineteen? Since he had been home he had noticed that it was impossible to tell the ages of the young girls, for they all had the same bright manes of hair, the same cool stare, the same mouth drawn in the same boring colour on the same little round face. These two girls wore cheap cotton frocks, short, probably shrunk with washing, and showing lots of bare leg. All right in summer, thought Stephen, to whom the unstockinged legs of the women of England, blue with December cold, splashed depressingly with mud as they scuffled after buses, had been one of the most unpleasant of the minor post-war shocks. But these little creatures had pretty sunburnt legs and arms, and as they hurried along, chattering like birds, their long soft hair flopped gently up and down on their shoulders. The taller of the two had bright red-gold hair, a wonderful colour, burning and rippling. Glancing at the car as she passed, she caught Stephen's eye and gave him a collected, impudent smile. I know why you are looking at me, her smile said, I know, I know, and I am delighted by it. She gave a little flick to the white bathing-suit she was carrying, and Stephen found himself smiling back. He twisted his head to have a last look at that amazingly lovely hair. She hastened away, away from him, a nymph fleeing back to the fountains and the uncut laurels. Stop! he wanted to cry to her. But she hurried along, not giving a damn, going to meet some wretched youth with a smooth face and a flat stomach, who would swim the crawl stroke the length of the Lido and hoist himself out, breathing as evenly as though he were stepping out of a punt. And suddenly Stephen realized that a car was hooting behind him. The traffic lights had changed, there he was blocking the way, staring like a fool after a red-headed child. Good Lord! he thought, the beginning of the end. He made a screaming mess of the gear change and shot forward, turning to the left of Queen Anne where the signpost pointed to Bridbury.

What an evening, he thought. Peace descended upon him as the houses thinned out, the groves of the stockbrokers' prunus and almond trees vanished, and now came the ruined castle among its rooks, the last funny little row of Regency houses which seemed to have been built here and forgotten, like a line of prim spinsters each holding a green iron bird-cage. Now he was clear of Ashton for at least another twelve hours. London had been infernally hot to-day. Miss Margesson's nose looked pinched and damp; when he went out to lunch the road gave slightly to the feet, sticky as warm toffee; the exhausts of all the throbbing buses and taxis rose on the glittering air and seemed to press down in a tight, acrid ceiling on the huge dome and the chimneys. Some time during the day, lighting a cigarette, a sort of disbelief had taken hold of him, and he had thought, Why does one do this? He had sat holding the lighter, so lost in thought that he forgot to put the flame out. He had suddenly wanted Laura to be there, so that he could ask her if she did not agree that it was supremely silly. But when he wanted to ask her something, she was never there, and when he got home she would be standing in the kitchen stirring something, a smudge of flour across her face which she would raise abstractedly to his kiss. Yes, she would say, listening abstractedly, Yes, darling, and suddenly an expression of anxiety would curdle her air of attention, she would whip open the oven door and snatch out some dish, planting it on the top of the stove with the sigh of relief of a runner tumbling into the tape. There seemed to be few of the old quiet moments for talking. All through their meal they would be jumping up and down. In the old days food appeared before one punctually and pleasantly, an illusion produced with no creaking trap doors or flashing of mirrors, the digestion and the mind could work calmly together, but now there was always this infernal jumping up and down. Perhaps Laura was not particularly clever about it. For he could not help noticing that the house was getting every day more and more like a last year's bird's nest beginning to crumble and fall away dustily from the eaves. Laura and old Prout did their best, no doubt, but grey fluff lurked under the beds; when he pulled out a book last night a pressed spider and a few strands of cordy, cobwebby stuff fluttered from between the pages. Oh *dear*, said Laura, but the trouble was that she did not really mind. Coming from the Herriot home where the very silver seemed to form fours on the gleaming mahogany, she had the oddest Bohemian streak of not caring, of being quite prepared to perch happily as a bird among a mess which would set his own teeth on edge. And Victoria, his daughter, so obviously took after Laura in that way. She was hopelessly untidy. Only this morning – he frowned – he had found the bathroom floor soaking wet, a damp towel thrown carelessly into the basin, and on the glass shelf, leering at him, the frightful wire thing which she wore round her front teeth. He stopped frowning, he had to smile when he remembered the irritated yelp he had let out, and the cool, injured little way in which she had said Sorry, taken the beastly object and scooped it into her mouth. The sideways flicker of her fair lashes, the way in which her glance had, for a second, taken him in from top to toe, standing there yattering in his dressing-gown, was a sudden adult imitation of somebody else giving a quelling look to an inferior. Was it her grandmother, Mrs. Herriot? When he had gone away she had been a tow-headed baby clasping a yellow duck. Now she was a square little girl, watching him, summing him up from an already chosen position, already taking out of the funny box of inherited possessions the sort of adult family mask which later she would be able to adopt at will. There goes my daughter, he had thought, feeling helpless, positively helpless, as he stood at the bathroom door and watched her skipping downstairs and, almost directly, heard floating up from the unfresh stillness of the unopened room the hideously clear one, two, three of her determined practising.

But Laura – he returned to Laura. Last night when they were undressing to go to bed, it had suddenly struck him how frightfully tired she looked. Outside the open windows the long summer twilight had come at last, bats whirled up and down against the glimmering green sky, some scent in the shadowy jungle garden, tobacco flower or stock, still floated up, faithfully sweet. 'It looks like a fine day to-morrow,' Laura said. She was sitting before her lighted dressing-table, brushing her hair. She wore her old blue dressing-gown, and she looked frightfully tired. He had caught sight of her reflection in the glass suddenly, sharp with the very slight distortion which a mirror gives. There she was, practically grey-haired at thirty-eight – why, he remembered his own mother, who must have been older than that at the time, with ropes and coils of dark hair almost without a grey hair. She had seemed younger, as he remembered, than Laura did now when she used to have lunch in his rooms at Cambridge. He remembered her once on a hot day, wearing a coquettish little hat trimmed with white birds, and looking a rather prettier elder sister to the young lady who, for Stephen's benefit, had accompanied her. But his Laura, tired and grey – there she sat, brushing her hair and saying something about the hens. He interrupted her.

'I'm going to give you a new hat,' he said. Of course it was a confused memory of his mother's coquettish white birds that had done it, but also there was a desire to give her something gay and frivolous, something new which she would put on and suddenly become Laura Herriot, the very tall, dreamy-looking girl in the water-green tulle dress, waltzing in the arms of someone in a pink coat. She is going to marry Philip Drayton, Connie Trehearne had told him as they rollicked round the room just behind the water-green tulle, but she had not, she had married him instead, to Mrs. Herriot's badly concealed disappointment. Thank God, he thought as he got into bed, thank God that Laura's mother, at any rate, has not descended on us lately. For he knew perfectly well that, in her subtle disparaging way, she blamed him for everything – for letting the European war happen, for letting Laura's hair go grey, for not being able to keep her in the comfort to which she had been accustomed, for growing middle aged. All this, and more, Stephen could read into one of Mrs. Herriot's unuttered sniffs. Thank God, he had thought, that for quite a while she has been apparently lying low and minding her own business down in St. Pol.

Laura had put down her brush, stared, and begun to laugh.

'How sweet of you,' she had said, 'but, darling, I don't wear hats any more, except on Sunday. And I've already got my —'

'No,' he had said firmly, 'I shall buy you a new hat. Come up and lunch with me one day soon, and we'll choose it.'

And to-day, on his way to lunch with someone at Boodle's, he had kept a sharp eye open for women wearing pretty hats. Extraordinary things they were, he thought, like tilted saucers filled with flowers, which their owners had perched above Britannic expressions of anxiety as though an infernal engine were ticking somewhere in the clouds of pale-blue and white veiling. He tried, and failed, to picture Laura in any of these. But while he was looking across the street at one as he walked up St. James's Street, someone called his name, and there was Nigel Fox who he had last seen in 1943. Old Nigel, fatter and redder than ever — good Lord, said Stephen, he was really tremendously glad to see him. It was true, he was tremendously glad, suddenly much happier, in some queer way, than he had been all day, or for days past. He could feel the mysterious lightness of his heart, the wonderful bounding of his spirits, just because he was standing beaming into old Nigel's red harvest moon of a face. It was a curious relief, as though suddenly there was nothing to explain, nothing to try and tell, because here was someone who knew it all. We know all about it, old cock, Nigel's grin seemed to say. And it seemed utterly ridiculous that he had not tried to get hold of him before! Utterly ridiculous! Where had he been all this time? Well, said Nigel, just around. Getting himself married for one thing.

'No!' said Stephen. 'Not that dark girl, what's-her-name, Ruth? A nurse, wasn't she?'

No, said Nigel, looking annoyed, not in the least that dark girl, what's-her-name, Ruth. Somebody very different. He explained.

'Bring her down for the week-end,' said Stephen grandly.

'You're still down at – where was it? – Wealding, wasn't it?' Nigel asked.

And old so-and-so, and this name and that – they began walking aimlessly together, the wrong way for Stephen to go, as they talked. The day was amazingly lovely. The hot sunshine was delicious, the people went by looking happy and relaxed. Look here, said Stephen, come and lunch.

'No, damn it, I forgot,' he said. 'I'm lunching with Baxter.'

'I've got a date too,' Nigel said, looking at his watch.

'Let's lunch next Monday,' Stephen said.

But suddenly old Nigel became vague. He couldn't lunch on Monday. Wednesday – well, could he ring Stephen? He got out a notebook and took down the number. They would certainly lunch soon, or better still, dine, if Stephen would stay in town for the night. He wrote down the number very large and distinct as though its largeness and distinctness ought somehow to reassure Stephen. He smote Stephen on the shoulder.

'Haven't changed a bit,' he said fondly.

But it wasn't true of either of them. They were different. Evasiveness came down like a shadow over Nigel's crimson face; he tapped his breast on the spot where he had stowed away his notebook, cried, 'I'll ring you!' and lumbered off into the sunshine. Stephen had a feeling that he would never see him again. Stop! he wanted to cry to Nigel Fox as, this evening, he wanted to cry to the red-headed nymph fleeing away to her laurels. There was Nigel lumbering away from him, disappearing among the fine shaving-brushes, the Chippendale bookcases, the fishing-rods, the glossy boots, the Georgian bow windows of St. James's Street. He vanished, he was swallowed up. After a minute, Stephen Marshall went on to lunch with Baxter.

All the same, it lasted, the lightness of heart, in slightly diminished form right up to the evening. After lunch, it had seemed highly probable that Nigel would ring him up. They must lunch, they would dine, he would come down to Wealding to stay and bring the girl who was not in the least Ruth. The feeling that they would never meet again was nonsense. To-night at dinner, thought Stephen, he would tell Laura about the meeting. She would remember old Nigel from his letters. There was so much to tell her this evening – Nigel, the preposterous hats in London, the way in which he had suddenly missed her in the middle of the long, hot day. Perhaps he might even be able to tell her that, if they stopped jumping up and down long enough. He felt awfully happy, driving home in the peace of the splendid evening. He had turned off the Bridbury road at the crossroads, and now the land on either side of the low hedges resumed its quiet lyric metre. Somebody's white pony was grazing in a field surrounded by huge oaks weighed down with heavy, soft-looking planes of foliage, the eternal Stubbs in the eternal Constable. On an evening like this all the great truths which had ever been stated about an English summer day seemed to come so freshly into the mind. And he found himself glancing from time to time at Barrow Down, the old hill towering over the fields and the little villages. An ice-blue shadow lay on its wooded lower slopes, giving its crown a look of Alpine loneliness and purity. How often he had thought of it while he was away, at all sorts of odd moments. In some peculiar way it had come to mean England for him, and his love of England, which was the reason why he was stuck here waiting for the next big bang, if it ever happened, and why Laura would never pick vivid blue trumpets off the picket fence of a white house in a strange land. However he might feel in moments of gloom, that was the reason. And it was something which Laura would never really understand, bless her heart, for women loved people, things, places, but not an idea, a vague shape somehow embodied in one rabbit-tunnelled old hill. He kept on glancing up at Barrow Down over the shag of wild roses and blackberry flowers. He must find time one day soon to get up there, to look at the view from the top. If ever I get a moment from the damned garden and the rest of the chores I'll walk up there, he thought.

He drove through Wealding. He looked at it affectionately, his village, the church, the little houses, men gardening quietly among the bean rows. He felt extraordinarily happy. When the car turned in at his gate, when he had backed it into the garage, just grazing old Voller's tricycle, he could hardly wait to get out and find Laura. He grabbed his hat and paper off the back seat and made off like an impetuous boy. The front door stood open. 'Laura!' he called. Silence. The house seemed very still. A rug was pushed askew, a music case had been thrown on the hall table and had come open, showering loose sheets of music and what looked like a damp little brown paper parcel of something on the floor. 'Laura!' he called again, but already the moment had been slightly flawed, her answer from the distant room or the far corner of the garden would not make up for the quite surprisingly sharp pang of disappointment. 'Yes, darling,' he would hear her calling faintly in a moment, and she would come in, smiling, saying that she had had no idea, the vague creature, that it was quite so late.

Instead, Victoria said over the edge of the stairs, 'She's not

166

back yet.' She came down towards him, step by step. 'I can't think where she's gone,' Victoria said. Collapsed, the moment hopelessly ruined and never to be revived, he stood in the middle of the hall staring up at her.

XIX

By nine o'clock Stephen was beginning to feel rather anxious.

His first impulse had been irritability. He gazed at Victoria and was struck by her extremely dishevelled appearance. Suddenly the lightness of heart started up by meeting Nigel Fox left him and he felt hot and tired, he knew that his first feeling had been right and that Nigel would not telephone. He dropped his hat on a chair and said to Victoria, 'Oughtn't you to be in your bath?'

'I'm running it,' she said, and he heard, far away upstairs, the splash of water running into the tub.

'She was going over to try and find Stuffy,' said Victoria.

'So she was. Well, she'll be back soon, I expect.'

Victoria disappeared. He stood for a moment irresolutely looking round him, then he began to wander from room to room, as though hoping Laura had left a footprint or perhaps a message on the pincushion to account for her absence. The rooms gave no clue, but the air was close; he opened the windows, letting out a bee who was crawling anxiously on the drawing-room panes. Everything looked unnaturally neat – ah yes, it was old Prout's day to come and bang the carpet sweeper against the chair legs. She had plumped up the cushions on the shabby Knole sofa and had just slightly changed the position of all Laura's Staffordshire figures on the bookshelves, but had she –? He ran a finger along the top of the books and, as usual, brought it away grubby, and the lampshades looked grey. The room had been redecorated at a time when it was fashionable to have everything 'off-white,' a colouring which now sounded somewhat sardonic. We ought to sell it, he thought, looking gloomily round. It's too big for Laura to manage, it's getting her down, and we'd never get a better price than we would now. Bellamy might like it. Only this morning in the train he had been saying that Hunter's Lodge was too small for them. The thought of Bellamy sitting here, crossing his legs and complacently fondling his little moustache, was oddly depressing. No, damn it, he thought, let's hold on a little longer and see if things improve. And it suddenly struck him as preposterous how dependent he and his class had been on the anonymous caps and aprons who lived out of sight and worked the strings. All his life he had expected to find doors opened if he rang, to wake up to the soft rattle of curtain rings being drawn back, to find the fires bright and the coffee smoking hot every morning as though household spirits had been working while he slept. And now the strings had been dropped, they all lay helpless as abandoned marionettes with nobody to twitch them. All the same, he'd be damned if he would sell the house to Bellamy!

He wandered out into the garden. The weeds looked as though they had battened and fattened on the heat of the day, they were surely worse than they had been this morning. He took an irritable stride into the middle of a rose bed, bent and yanked at a monstrous dandelion which had seeded into impertinent puffs of silky floss there among the poor Étoile de

Hollandes. The ground was too hard. The root merely broke off with a juicy snap, staining his hand, and he straightened up in disgust. Had Laura, he wondered, done anything about young Porter? Probably not, for she had an awful memory. He went down to the kitchen garden to see how that old fool Voller was getting along. The raspberries were netted all right, the jays were making an outraged squawking from the cherry trees, and the old man was hoeing at the far end beyond the asparagus bed. Stephen had meant to go along and shout one or two questions at him, but for some reason he stayed in the archway watching Voller, whose back was turned. The old man went on hoeing, very slowly, moving his spidery thin arms back and forth. He was bent as a thorn bush, the back of his neck was earth-coloured and seamed with deep lines and furrows, as though all the sorrows and cares of Voller's life had somehow gone to his neck. The sound of his hoe breaking up the earth was oddly soothing, the sight of him working away quietly in the lovely evening light gave Stephen a peaceful feeling, he could not have explained why. Why worry? he thought. All will be well. And yet he had not the faintest idea why looking at old Voller, scratching away like a patient old mole at a few square feet of England, should make him feel suddenly peaceful. All he knew was, he did not feel like breaking up the moment by bellowing into Voller's ear. He turned away, lighting a cigarette, and went back to the house.

Someone was moving plates in the kitchen. He went in quickly, saying, 'Hallo! You're back!' But it was Victoria, who must have bathed with extraordinary rapidity, and was now, in dressing-gown and pyjamas, bustling back and forth from the dining-room.

'I've laid the table,' she said, 'and I've put something in the oven. It looks like fish.'

She had the flushed and triumphant air all women wear when meeting the sudden emergency, as though drawing from it a mysterious source of pleasure. He looked at her respectfully.

'Thanks,' he said.

'You won't have potatoes,' she said; 'I'm afraid there wasn't time.'

'That's all right,' he said meekly.

'Will you start?' she asked. 'I expect you're awfully hungry, aren't you? Probably Mummy has popped in to see someone. You know what she is about time,' she added with an amused, social manner – was it a gruesome echo of Mrs. Herriot again? Mesmerized, he followed her flapping slippers into the dining-room. She had laid the table profusely, adding the silver candlesticks which they never used, several ashtrays and an empty sugar-sifter.

'I do hope it's done,' she said when they had taken the fish out of the oven and brought it into the dining-room.

'It looks perfect,' Stephen said.

She beamed.

'What about you?' he asked. 'Aren't you going to have some with me?'

'I don't think so,' she said. 'I'll bring in a glass of milk, just to keep you company – I think there's some milk over. I ate such an awful lot at the Watsons'. Oh, Mrs. Watson sent you some cream cheese – it's on the sideboard.' And there it was, looking small and damp in the middle of a huge plate.

Victoria, coming back with her milk, said suddenly, 'Perhaps she met a bull.'

'Who?' asked Stephen, startled.

'Mummy. I saw a perfectly immense bull to-day – it belonged to Mr. Watson.'

She began telling him about the Watsons' farm. Her bath or

the heat of her exertions had given her a damp, rosy look. She's going to be pretty, he thought, when she gets that damned coil of wire out of her mouth. He listened, nodding, thinking with amusement what it would be like to have a pretty daughter on his hands. Before they knew where they were, she would be a long-legged thing like that red-headed minx he had seen in Ashton, hurrying away, away, disappearing among the uncut laurels. She still looked very small, though, sitting drinking her milk at one side of the long table which they had bought in the old days when there were always people to dinner, people staying, never a minute to themselves. A long, positively patriarchal table. We should have had more children, thought Stephen, swallowing fish pie and looking round the empty places. Eight children, four boys, four girls. That is what we should have done, before the blighting weather set in which makes one worry to death over the future of even this solitary little object sitting licking milk of its downy upper lip. He would have liked a boy. It was locked up in his soul; he had never let Laura, even, suspect how much he would have liked a boy. But one worried desperately, desperately. All will be well, old Voller had mysteriously stated to the earth, bound in some ancient alliance in the greenish light between the asparagus bed and the tall hazels. But I don't know, I don't know, thought Stephen.

'Couldn't we,' Victoria was asking, 'have a cow, don't you think? Just one? She could live perfectly well in the orchard, if you made her a little house.'

She was looking at him in suspense, hanging on his answer. It was obviously of enormous importance. He pushed back his plate.

'Well,' he said, 'let's think. There's the milking of it, in the first place –'

He had not said no. He was discussing the question with her, in a gratifying, reasonable adult way. She seemed about to blow up, she turned so pink, and then she gave him a deep, soft look of love, so breathtaking, so utterly delicious that he felt he would promise her a dozen cows if she would often look at him like that.

'We could make our own butter,' she said. 'You could always have cream cheese like this.' She scrambled up and set it before him with a flourish.

Afterwards, when she had gone up to bed, he began to feel just a little anxious. What on earth had happened to Laura? She had gone, of course, on that wretched old bicycle of hers. It had no brakes, it was obviously due to buckle up at any moment, he had told her only the other day that Jukes had got some perfectly decent new bikes down in the village. But she preferred to hang on to the old rattletrap, and now look what had happened, it had let her down. It had punctured or lost its chain somewhere in the maze of lanes at the foot of Barrow Down. That was the best that could have happened. At the worst, she was now lying senseless somewhere, in a ditch, crumpled up in a heap on the road. He would go out in the car and look for her, he thought. He went upstairs to fetch a new packet of cigarettes out of his dressing-room, and was stopped by Victoria's voice calling him.

He went into her room.

'I've been sick,' she said.

She was sitting up in bed, looking deadly pale.

'Hold on,' he said. 'I'll get a basin.'

'I'm afraid it's too late,' she gasped politely.

'Well, a – a sponge.' He bolted from the room.

For the next few minutes he was very busy. Victoria leant

against him, her forehead was damp and glistening. He kissed it, and she sighed.

'I knew I'd eaten too much at the Watsons',' she said.

'I expect the heat had something to do with it, darling,' he said.

She lay quietly, twiddling one of the buttons on his coat. She sighed again.

'I feel better now,' she said.

'We'd better do something about your bed,' he said.

What a day, he thought, rummaging about in the linen-cupboard. He found clean sheets and a pillowcase, he brought them back and put them on Victoria's bed, he hunted fresh pyjamas out of the drawer and peeled her out of the old ones.

'Poor old baby,' he said when he had got her tucked up again and she lay there, placidly watching him, the pink colour already draining back healthily into her face. By this time he was the one who was feeling slightly queazy. He bent to kiss her.

'Don't go,' she said.

'I must,' he said. 'I'm going to have a look outside the gate and see if I can see Mummy coming.'

'You don't think anything's happened, do you?' she asked.

She eyed him narrowly over the bedclothes. 'Our darling Mother, from Aggie and Flo' – with a sudden pang of fright she remembered the raw-looking heap of new earth, the flowers dangling their black-edged messages. It happened to people, they died, you could run into the house and call their names again and again, but only old Nobody would answer.

'Good Lord, no,' Stephen said, mockingly reassuring.

She put out her arms and gave him a huge strangling kiss. She was only a baby after all, she believed things with beautiful ease. Then she fell back on the pillow, and he had a feeling that she would be asleep almost as soon as he was out of the room. He went along to the bathroom and washed his hands and fetched the packet of cigarettes. It was really not any good to go and see if he could meet Laura, on second thoughts, for there were two ways that she might come and they could easily miss each other. He went downstairs again and cleared away the supper things. The cat sat watching him, with that insufferable feline air of knowing everything, of being able to speak if she liked. He dumped the china and silver in the sink. He really could not tackle washing-up tonight. And suddenly for the first time he thought of the gypsy fellow. Was he all right? No one knew very much about him except that he lived in the old railway-coach shack up on Barrow Down. If she's not back in half an hour, thought Stephen, I'll take the car straight up there and have a look around. Perhaps later on he ought to ring up the Wealding police station. No, really, he thought, this is too farcical. Dodge, their policeman, was such a pompous old fool, cycling round the village very slowly as though the law was a steel ramrod stuffed down the back of his tunic. Stephen could imagine him coming to the telephone in the square red box of a police station, embowered in Dorothy Perkins roses and ear-wigs, and taking it all down slowly and laboriously in a black notebook. 'Larst seen at breakfast, eight fifteen – ay – em –' Ah, what nonsense, thought Stephen. For it was only a puncture, nothing but a puncture.

He went out again. He could not settle down to anything. The evening was consolingly lovely, and he remembered that dusk, when there would be time to think of Dodge, was still some way ahead. In this last magnificent burst of light, people at the sea would still be bathing, the few remaining children would be trailing home along the sand dunes, lovers would sit hand in hand on the cliffs watching the fishing-boat creep along the glittering pathway of the sinking sun. It was dropping fast, the sun, but it still showered the earth superbly with light, denying the watch on Stephen's wrist. Only a little owl spoke thinly, huskily, among the trees, as though impatient for night. The ducks still waddled in the paddock, busily searching the ground, not thinking of bed. He leant on the fence to watch them. They stopped, frozen, eyeing him with alarm. Then as he did not move, they began timidly and then forgetfully to potter and flap once more.

He leant against the fence. What could have happened to Laura? He felt suddenly irritable, he did not believe about the puncture, she had simply forgotten about the time, that was all. She was hopeless, absolutely hopeless! He remembered past occasions when she had forgotten the time and kept him waiting at railway stations, drinking lonely beers to while away the minutes in pub bars, kicking about one freezing winter day in Salisbury Cathedral where he felt his toes turning cold as Saxon stone. Then she would drift in, smiling, unrepentant, explaining that she had just picked up a book, or started a conversation with someone, or followed a fascinating little street which had somehow led her a few miles out of her way. He absolutely shuddered to think how she and Victoria had got along while he was away. Meals on trays, all the clocks wrong, and the worst of it would be, nobody would mind in the least. And suddenly he remembered the telephone bill which had been such a nasty shock at breakfast. Of course there had been no mistake, the horrid total was correct, and it was certainly mostly Laura's doing. Neither she nor her mother had the slightest telephone conscience. They would ramble away by the hour, without a thought of the appalling sum which in time he and the poor old Colonel would have to face. Laura had no idea of money. What an upbringing, he thought, for the kind of life in which we are all floundering now, and likely to flounder. She was really impossible!

But at the same time he knew that this was just a bluff put up to hide his growing panic. Without her, everything was dust and ashes. He knew that perfectly well, watching the ducks roll and pause and suddenly rear on end to explore with their beaks under a wing feather. When she came back – for she must come, there was some perfectly ordinary reason for her absence – he would be so relieved that his temper might flare up, he might ask her angrily where she had been, giving them all such a scare, even to the point of thinking of telephoning Dodge. Or he might simply say, for once, that he loved her, that without her everything was dust and ashes. He did not know. The little owl called again. Soon it will be night, soon, soo-o-oon. He straightened up and swung round from the fence so abruptly that the ducks, who had been exploring close to him, ran some little way before they felt emboldened to turn and watch him out of sight.

XX

Stuffy heard the footsteps and growled. The young man in the blue shirt did not hear her growl. He was going downhill at a brisk pace by a track a little below them. He was feeling extraordinarily happy, for he had had a wonderful day walking over Barrow Down to Grimsditch, on to Pike Castle and the tiny Norman church at Stormell. Now, by a slightly different way, he was returning by Barrow Down again to catch his train from Bridbury. He had eaten bread and cheese, sitting on a white bench in a little pub garden, where the beery cool smell of the sanded bar floated out of the window and joined the smell of the honeysuckle growing up a rustic arch above him. A pickled onion had fallen in the middle of the second page of *Ode to Melancholy*, but it had left no mark. His neck flamed, it would be painful later on. He felt very happy. It was the day he had been planning for himself ever since he got out of the Army, and it had kept fine for him, a perfect summer day at last after all the bad weather. Whistling softly to himself, he disappeared down the rough grass slope among the thorn bushes.

Stuffy's growl had woken Laura. She sat up, feeling cramped, pushing back her hair. I must have dropped off, she thought guiltily. But for how long? She had no idea. Oceans of wonderful sleep seemed to have rolled over her, she had rocked and floated deliciously in endless caverns booming with the surf of Mrs. Vyner's music. The land had sung, she remembered that. She had heard it singing under her ear, pressed against the milky little flowers. Now she could tell from the deepening shadow, the wider glacier of cold blue which had slid down the slope into the valley, that it was really getting late. The great bowl below her was slightly misted over, and a fluff of beautiful pink clouds, a feather-bed of flamingo down, hung in the sky. Good heavens! she thought in alarm. Victoria will have got home long ago, Stephen will have got home, they will be wondering what on earth has become of me.

She sprang to her feet, or tried to spring to her feet, but she was awfully stiff. She staggered and stood for a moment, her head spinning stupidly. I am glad I got to the top, she thought, looking dizzily down into the great misty bowl. But now she wanted to be down in it, to be part of it, to be home. She wanted to run in, calling their names, to find Stephen and say to him – what? Something that had come into her mind just before she fell asleep, though it did not really matter. She was feeling so extremely happy.

Stuffy was barking excitably, relieved that the long rest was over. 'Come on then,' said Laura, stooping to pick up her scattered belongings.

And she began to run down the hill.